IT TAKES MORE THAN GOOD GRADES TO GRADUATE FROM CENTRAL ACADEMY . . .

Discover the chilling adventures that shadow the halls and stalk the students of **TERROR ACADEMY!**

LIGHTS OUT

School reporter Mandy Roberts investigates the suspicious past of the new assistant principal. The man her widowed mother plans to marry . . .

STALKER

A tough punk comes back to Central with one requirement to complete: vengeance . . .

SIXTEEN CANDLES

Kelly Langdon discovers there's more to being popular than she thought—like staying alive . . .

SPRING BREAK

It's the vacation from hell. And it's up to Laura Hollister to save her family. And herself . . .

THE NEW KID

There's something about the new transfer student. He's got a deadly secret . . .

STUDENT BODY

No one's safe at Central—when a killer roams the halls . . .

This book also contains a preview of the next exciting book in the TERROR ACADEMY series by Nicholas Pine: **SCIENCE PROJECT.**

 S0-DJM-162

TERROR ACADEMY

NIGHT SCHOOL

NICHOLAS PINE

BERKLEY BOOKS, NEW YORK

NIGHT SCHOOL

A Berkley Book / published by arrangement with
the author

PRINTING HISTORY
Berkley edition / January 1994

ISBN: 0-425-14151-9

BERKLEY®
Berkley Books are published by The Berkley Publishing Group,
200 Madison Avenue, New York, New York 10016.
BERKLEY and the "B" design
are trademarks belonging to Berkley Publishing Corporation.

PRINTED IN THE UNITED STATES OF AMERICA

10 9 8 7 6 5 4 3 2 1

This book is dedicated to Nicole Smith of Madison, New Hampshire.

NIGHT SCHOOL

ONE

Stacey Linden ran the blunt end of the red lipstick over her lips several times before she looked in the mirror. She pursed her lips in a mocking kiss, pretending that she was kissing the handsome boy from the afternoon soap opera that she taped and watched everyday when she got home from school. With her lips properly rouged, Stacey turned her attention to her eyelashes, brushing them with a heavy coat of mascara. She blinked a couple of times, checking out the reflection of her own deep blue eyes in the looking glass. Her skin was pale and smooth. Stacey never went to the beach like the rest of her friends. She avoided the sun because she didn't want to ruin her almost perfect complexion.

The seventeen-year-old Central Academy junior leaned back on the bench that rested in front of her vanity table. She studied the freshly plucked eyebrows that arched toward her smooth forehead. Stacey took a great deal of pride in her appearance. She was one of the most beautiful girls in the junior class at Central. No! *The* most beautiful, she thought.

Stacey smiled. It wasn't a sincere expression, but rather a winsome act to see how she looked with her lips parted just so. The smile quickly disappeared.

"Oh no!"

The lipstick had smeared onto Stacey's pearly-white teeth. She ran into her own private bathroom and brushed away the crimson color. When she came back to the mirror, she sat down and looked at herself again.

A sigh escaped between Stacey's full lips. She was a little bored. She had ditched school on this day because the junior class was taking a scholastic evaluation exam. Stacey never went in much for academics, even though Central Academy was known for being one of the best schools in all of New England.

"Stacey, honey?"

A slight rapping followed the pleasant voice. Stacey's mother had appeared at the door of her bedroom. Stacey took a deep breath because she knew she would have to lie to her mother.

"Come on in, Mom."

Madeline Linden came through the door and smiled at her only child. Stacey resembled her mother, although Mrs. Linden was darker and heavier. But they both had the same brown

hair, dense and streaked with reddish high-
lights that occurred naturally. Mrs. Linden's
tresses were also touched by strands of gray.

"Stacey," Mrs. Linden said in a concerned
tone, "it's almost ten o'clock. You're awfully late
for school."

"Uh, I don't have to be there until noon,"
Stacey lied, never glancing away from the sil-
very glass.

Mrs. Linden frowned. "Are you sure?"

"Uh-huh," Stacey replied, picking up the lipstick again. "Juniors are exempt from classes
today until twelve. They're having some sort of
senior assembly, something like that."

"I can call and check with the administration
at Central," Mrs. Linden challenged.

Stacey shrugged. "Go ahead, Mom. I don't
care. You want the number of the principal's
office? I know it by heart."

Mrs. Linden hesitated for a moment, then
said, "No, I trust you, honey."

Stacey had never been a straight-A student,
though she had always managed to pass her
courses at Central, maintaining a B average.
Still, her mother often wondered about Stacey's
study habits. Stacey never seemed to crack a
book. She was more interested in boys, clothes
and looking like a model from a glamour magazine. She hoped that her daughter would go on
to college one day, but Stacey had never even

mentioned furthering her education after she graduated from Central.

"Your dad and I are going out to dinner tonight," Mrs. Linden offered. "Would you like to come with us?"

Stacey exhaled, as if going out to dinner with her parents would be the most boring thing on earth. "Uh, no thanks, Mom. I can make something for myself."

"Are you sure, honey? I mean, we hardly ever see you anymore. Your dad would really like it if you came with us."

Stacey felt a little guilty about not spending more time with her father, Joseph Linden. He was the head of the Port City Planning Commission, and a possible candidate for mayor in a few years. Stacey wasn't exactly sure what her father did for a living, but she knew that he made big money and that she was able to spend quite a bit of it on herself. Stacey had a brand-new Geo Tracker sitting in the driveway. She had drifted away from her mother and father in the past year or so, since she had started driving and dating. Stacey's social life meant everything to her.

"Uh, I have a date tonight, Mom," Stacey replied. "Maybe later in the week."

Mrs. Linden's face registered matronly disapproval. "It's Monday, Stacey. You had a date last night. And the night before. If you—"

Stacey swung around on the vanity bench,

glaring at her mother. "Are you going back on our deal, Mom?"

Mrs. Linden blushed. "No, it's just—"

Stacey's voice was calm, calculated. "You and Dad said that if I keep a B average in my classes, that I can come and go as I please. I mean, I'm seventeen now. Isn't that right?"

Mrs. Linden sighed, "Stacey—"

"Just tell me, Mom, if you want to go back on our deal. I mean, I do have a B average. I never miss school unless I'm really sick. And I haven't been sick all year."

"It's only the end of October, Stacey," her mother said. "You still have another seven months of classes to go this year. If you want to go to college, you have to start taking your studies more seriously."

Stacey turned around, staring into the mirror again. "I do take them seriously. I'm just not a bookworm like you were, Mom. I like to have fun. And there's nothing wrong with that, not as long as I keep my grades up. Isn't that what we agreed to?"

Mrs. Linden sighed again. "All right, Stacey. I give up. I'm going to work."

Mrs. Linden also had a job with the city government of Port City, as the assistant director of the Municipal Parks and Recreation Department. She couldn't understand why her own daughter wasn't more serious about getting a college degree someday. She knew that Stacey was spoiled, and it was her own fault.

After her mother left, Stacey took a deep breath and exhaled. Why was her mother always on her case? Stacey had no intention of going to college. She had other plans after she blew off the dweebs and geeks at Central Academy.

Her deep blue eyes wandered to her image in the glass. With a vain gesture, she tossed her hair back over her shoulder. Then she struck a seductive pose, imitating the sultry models that she saw in fashion magazines.

"Don't blame me for being beautiful," she said to herself, repeating the words she had heard in a television commercial. "I was born like this, you see."

Gazing at her own lovely face, Stacey thought of the post-graduation plans she had made for herself: no college—she was going straight to New York to be a fashion model. She knew all about it from watching a documentary on television. She would simply walk into an agent's office and demand to be seen by the head of the agency. Surely he would recognize her natural beauty and talent. He'd turn her into the hottest model in the U.S. and then the entire world. She'd be more famous than Cindy Crawford or Linda Evangelista. Her face would be on every magazine cover, every television commercial and, eventually, a movie career would come her way.

Stacey loosened her terry cloth bathrobe, popping out her bare white shoulder. She struck various poses for the mirror—happy, sad, thoughtful, pouty. Twirling her hair in her hand, she piled it all on top of her head, winking at herself. Then she let the hair fall, spilling over her face. For a moment, she peered through the tresses with one eye, trying to look like a professional model.

"Ah, yes, Christian," she said, invoking the name of a hot young movie star, "I'd be delighted to have dinner with you. Tonight? Oh, I can't. I'm flying out to Paris in a couple of hours. Maybe when I get back. Leave your number with my secretary. Kiss kiss."

Stacey laughed haughtily, trying to effect an air of nonchalance. Rising from the vanity bench, she dropped her robe and bounced around her room, walking, slinking like a poster on the runway of a fancy fashion show. She was slender, beautiful, possessed of delicate white skin and perfect posture. How could she fail?

Why couldn't her mother see her talents? Mrs. Linden always came on with that stuff about college and books. Stacey didn't need any of it. As long as she could remember her lines from the movie script, she wouldn't even have to be able to read.

As the minutes ticked away on the clock, Stacey took her time getting ready for school. She tried on one outfit after another, pretending that she was the star of her own fashion show. By the time she settled on designer jeans, and white silk blouse and a leather jacket, it was almost time to go. The other juniors were probably finishing up their scholastic evaluation exams by now.

Stacey didn't look down on her classmates, she just found them sort of boring and immature. She had no close friends, just a few acquaintances and the boys she dated. Why did she need a bunch of geeky freinds? The other girls were jealous or afraid that Stacey might steal their dweebed-out boyfriends, as though she could even be bothered.

She hated jocks.

Cheerleading was a big waste of time.

Studying was for losers.

Stacey didn't need anyone but herself.

She just wanted to have a good time.

She had it made.

Or at least she thought she did.

TWO

Stacey backed out of the driveway in her lime-green Geo Tracker. The Jeep-like vehicle had a convertible top that was fixed up in the cool air of autumn. Stacey put the Tracker in gear and rolled toward the entrance of Prescott Estates, the fanciest neighborhood in Port City. It was almost noontime. Any minute now the bell from the North Church tower would ring, sending everyone in Port City to lunch.

With her sunglasses on, Stacey really did resemble a high-fashion model. She drove out of the neighborhood, turning right on Middle Road. At the first stoplight, a carload of sailors whistled and catcalled to her. Stacey just ignored them. Port City was a harbor town, always full of sailors from ports all over the world.

On the way to school, Stacey passed several landmarks that were well known throughout New England: Old Cemetery, a house where

John Paul Jones had once lived, North Church and Fair Common Park—places that made the quaint seaside town one of the most visited tourist stops during the summer. She detoured away from the main road so she could ride along the Tide Gate River, through a section of town known as Pitney Docks. It was a little run-down, but Stacey had always thought of Pitney Docks as a great place for a fashion photographer to have a shoot.

As she was turning back toward the main road, she heard the church bell pealing over the red-brick structures of the village. She stepped on the accelerator, rushing through the yellow caution light as the traffic signal changed. Stacey didn't want to be late, at least not for lunch. She had business to attend to at Central Academy.

She approached the school from Middle Road, turning down Rockbury Lane so she could get to the junior parking lot. Central Academy was a fairly new school, built in the boom of the eighties. The campus was large, sporting three classroom buildings, one for each class— sophomore, junior and senior. In the Port City school system, freshmen attended middle school, not high school.

Central also had a huge gymnasium, a library attached to the senior building, a domed swimming pool and a football stadium that also served as a place for the track-and-field events.

Stacey hated sports. She only took one year of physical education because it was required. She had her own exercise regimen and diet rules. Models had to attend to such things if they were going to make it in this cut throat business.

When Stacey saw that the junior lot was full, she parked in an empty space on the faculty side. After all, the teachers were already there for the day. It wasn't like she was taking someone's spot.

She hurried toward the middle of the Central campus. A large plaza sat at the hub of the school grounds, serving as a meeting place and lunch site for the students. The plaza was full on this gorgeous fall day. The juniors had finished their test and were outside, eating and discussing the rigors of the exam.

"Hey," someone said, "there's Stacey Linden. Stacey, you missed the exam."

"Big deal," Stacey muttered under her breath.

Stacey's dark blue eyes scanned the plaza, looking for a short-haired girl with glasses. "Where is she?" Stacey asked herself.

The girl was supposed to meet her right after twelve. Stacey had called her the night before to set it up. She hoped the little geek didn't let her down.

"Stacey, over here!"

The meek voice had come from behind her. Stacey turned to see Millie Johnson walking toward her. Millie wore a ratty dress and dirty sneakers. Her narrow green eyes were obscured by the thick lenses of horn-rimmed glasses.

"It's about time," Stacey said. "Do you have what I asked you for? All of it?"

Millie produced a thick envelope from her notebook. "It's all there. Your term paper and your math homework. What are you going to do about the math test?"

Stacey shrugged. "I'll cheat like I always do. How much do I owe you?"

Millie shifted anxiously on her feet. "Uh, didn't we say fifty dollars?"

"Sure," Stacey replied offhandedly. "Fifty bucks. Here—"

Digging into her jeans, she took out five ten-dollar bills, money she had saved from her allowance. Money meant very little to Stacey. She was going to have a ton of it someday when she was a big-time model. She'd have it all—a townhouse in New York, a Beverly Hills palace and a villa on the Riviera.

Millie took the money from her. "Thanks. My mom and I really need the money. My little brother has to have an operation next month. He's—"

"Yeah, sure, whatever," Stacey replied.

She walked away from Millie, leaving the dorky girl to count the money. Stacey had little time for dweebs like Millie. After all, she had *paid* to have her school work done for her.

Wasn't that enough without having to listen to her complain?

As she strode across campus, everyone called and waved to Stacey. They pretended to be friendly to her, but after she had passed, they made comments behind her back. Stacey didn't hear what they were really saying.

"Hi, Stacey . . . what a stuck-up—"

"Looking good, Stacey . . . and she knows it—"

"You missed the test, Stacey . . . she misses everything except her own reflection in the mirror—"

Stacey just cruised by her classmates with her perfect nose tilted slightly in the air. She *wanted* them to think about her, even if it wasn't exactly good. They'd all be envious when she was on the cover of *Cosmopolitan*. She figured she'd best get used to the notoriety.

Stopping in front of a group of junior girls, Stacey focused her blue eyes on a blonde-haired girl. "Hi, Priss, have you seen Derek today?"

Prissy Young, the co-captain of the cheerleading squad, gazed back at Stacey with narrow green eyes. "No, I haven't seen him. He was probably taking the test like the rest of us. I didn't see *you* there."

Stacey flashed a catty smile. "No, you didn't."

She moved on, searching in the crowd for Derek Barton, one of the boys she dated from time to time. Derek wasn't her boyfriend, but he had plenty of money, a nice car and the where-withal to take Stacey to fancy places on their dates. Stacey hated the usual movie/burger-joint outings suffered by other teenagers. She liked going to expensive restaurants, local theater productions and the occasional jaunt to Boston for a big concert by a top band like Poison or Guns N' Roses.

She kept asking for Derek in the plaza, but no one had seen him. He had been at the test earlier, one person replied, but he had disappeared. Stacey wondered if he had ditched the rest of the school day. She'd be angry if he left without her. They could have spent the afternoon shopping together.

"Have you seen Derek?" she asked a dark-haired girl.

Belinda Wright, president of the junior class, shook her head and batted the lashes of her brown eyes. "No. What's the matter, Stacey? Did he break loose from your leash?"

Stacey grimaced. "What happened to your hair, Belinda? It looks awful."

Belinda grimaced back. "I had a permanent. Everybody likes it, even Derek."

Stacey arched one of her perfect eyebrows. "A perm? It looks like you dipped your head in a vat of toxic waste."

"Ha-ha!" Belinda replied sarcastically.

But Stacey was already moving again, looking for Derek. She finally found him in the cafeteria, sipping from a carton of milk. Derek was really handsome, tall, tanned, with blue eyes and long black hair that hung to his shoulders. He wasn't a jock or a brain, even though he was fairly intelligent. Stacey liked him because he was a little dangerous and he played in a heavy-metal band on the weekends.

Stacey frowned when she saw that Derek was sitting with another girl—Jenny Martin. Jenny, like a lot of other girls in the junior class, had a crush on Derek. Stacey hurried to the table, sitting down next to Derek and sliding her arm over his broad shoulders.

"Hi, handsome," she said in a breathy tone.

Derek grinned at her. "Looking good, Stace. Missed you at the big test this morning."

"I don't do tests," Stacey replied.

Jenny gazed narrow-eyed at the interloper who had suddenly stolen Derek from her. "Hi, Stacey," she said coldly.

Stacey wasted no time leveling her disapproving expression on the sandy-haired pretender to Derek's attentions. "Uh, Jenny, I think I hear your mother calling you."

Jenny bristled, her brown eyes growing wide. "Derek!"

He waved her off. "See ya, Jenny. Later."

"No, you won't," Stacey said.

Red-faced, Jenny rose from the table and stormed off, glancing back over her shoulder to blast daggers at Stacey.

Derek turned to peer into Stacey's dark blue eyes. "You're looking great today. Any chance for a kiss?"

Stacey gave a haughty laugh. "No, you'll mess up my lipstick."

Derek ran his hand over her shoulder, massaging gently. "It was really hot in my van the other night. Nobody ever kissed me like that before. I thought something *else* was going to happen."

"It almost did," Stacey teased. "But it's never going to happen if you keep hanging out with dweebs like Jenny Martin."

Derek shrugged, brushing back his long, thick hair. "Hey, what can I do? I'm sitting here and she sits down."

"You can tell her to take a hike," Stacey replied.

Derek sighed and shook his head. "You know, Stacey, you always hand me this jealous routine, like we're going together or something. But you never want to make a commitment to me. I mean, what's the story?"

Stacey feigned anger and dismay. "*I'm* not the one who wants to make a commitment? Every time I see you, you've got some bimbo wrapped around you. I mean, what's *that* about?"

Derek looked away, a hurt expression on his handsome face. "That's not fair," he replied. "You date other guys."

"And you date other girls." Stacey challenged. "Don't you?"

He glanced back at her, peering into her eyes. "I don't want to, Stacey. You know that. Any time you want to make it official, I'll tell everyone that we're going together."

Stacey exhaled, shaking her head. "I don't know, Derek. Guys like you always have a lot of girls around."

He blushed, growing irritated. "What's that supposed to mean?"

"Well, you're in a band," Stacey went on. "And I can't always be there when you want me to come to your gigs."

"So?"

"Well, it's just hard for me to trust you. You're really a hunky guy. The girls are always after you."

"But I don't want all the other girls," Derek insisted. "I want you. I mean, we talked, you know. About going to New York together when we graduate. I'll have my own band and you can do the modeling thing. Isn't that it?"

Stacey grimaced again. They had talked about it, but she wasn't sure she wanted Derek along for the ride. After all, the music business was a tough nut to crack. She didn't have confidence that he would make it big, the way *she* planned to make it big.

"So what's it gonna be?" Derek asked.

Stacey sighed. "I don't want to talk about this now, Derek—"

He jumped to his feet, backing away from the table, knocking over the chair. "You're just a tease," he said to her.

Stacey shook her head. "Derek, don't—"

"No, I mean it," Derek railed, "you don't really want me but you don't want anyone else to have me. You want me to stick around like some puppy dog."

"Derek, you're overreacting—"

"Aw, forget it," he said. "I've had it with you, Stacey. Give me a call if you decide to grow up."

Derek stomped away from the table, leaving Stacey by herself. Everyone had seen them arguing. Stacey straightened her posture, watching as Derek joined Jenny Martin again.

"What a jerk," she muttered to herself.

The bell rang, signaling the end of the lunch period. Stacey rose from the table and started for the hallway. She had to go to math class, where she would hand in the homework that Millie had done for her. As far as she was concerned, Derek was history as long as he acted like a child.

As she moved toward her classroom, Stacey was thinking about the other boys she had been dating. There was Rick, but he attended Port City Community College, so she didn't see him that often. She really only dated Rick because she wanted to be able to say she was going out with a college guy. The other boy was Jeff, a senior at Central. But lately, Jeff had been sort of cold to her, giving her the same commitment speech that had come out of Derek's mouth.

Why did boys have to be so immature? she wondered as she sat down at the desk in her math class. After all, Stacey didn't care one bit about going steady. It was crazy how the other girls went gah-gah over the boys when they offered their class rings or their letter sweaters. Stacey didn't want to feel like she *belonged* to someone else. She was a human being, not some guy's private property.

Stacey turned her attention to the homework that Millie had prepared for her. Stacey was careful to make sure that some of the problems were wrong. She didn't want a perfect grade-point average. If she got straight A's, her parents would always be expecting her to come home with a flawless report card.

For nearly all of her schooling, Stacey had relied on others to do her work for her. She paid them now, but in elementary and middle school she had relied on her desserts at lunch or candy bars and the occasional toy to bring in the homework. She had learned to cheat on tests, to get by with B's and the odd C. Whenever her grades dipped below a B average, she would turn in a couple of A-caliber homework papers to bring up the grades.

Stacey was good at her subterfuge. She had

never been caught in all her years of cheating. The teachers were downright stupid. They didn't notice as long as she maintained the appearance of doing the work. And her system allowed her to stay out late on school nights, dating or doing whatever she wanted.

When the bell rang, the teacher, Mr. Bradock, appeared behind his desk, gazing at the class through thick glasses. "All right, pass up your homework everyone." He smiled at Stacey, who sat in the first row as part of her scheming.

Stacey smiled back, passing along the homework that she had paid for with her allowance money.

It was all so perfect.

She had no idea that her life was about to take some drastic turns that would change her forever.

THREE

Halfway through the math class, the loudspeaker crackled behind the teacher's desk. "Would Stacey Linden please report to the vice-principal's office? Stacey Linden, please report to the vice-principal's office immediately."

Stacey squinted at the speaker, not sure she had heard right. She had been leaning on her hand, pretending to pay attention to Mr. Bradock's lecture. Some of the other students giggled when they heard Stacey's name.

Mr. Bradock seemed concerned about the announcement. "Uh, Stacey, that's you."

"But I—"

He nodded at her. "Go on, Stacey. It sounds like something important. You'd better hurry. And take your books with you."

Stacey was steaming as she left the room. What was going on anyway? A call to the vice-principal's office always meant trouble. And she had never been in trouble before.

She left the junior classroom building, walking across the campus to the administration offices, which were located in the adjacent building for the senior classes. When she strolled into the office of Harlan Kinsley, vice-principal of Central Academy, Stacey was taken aback to see that Jenny Martin was the student assistant on duty at the desk. Jenny smiled haughtily, like she had suddenly scored one against Stacey.

Stacey glared at her. "Did you have something to do with this, Jenny? Because if you did—"

Jenny shrugged, still grinning. "I don't know a thing about it," she replied. "Mr. Kinsley just asked me to take the announcement to the front office."

Stacey glanced toward the closed door that bore the vice-principal's name in big black letters. "Well, I want to see him now and get this over with. What's it about, anyway?"

"I told you, I don't know," Jenny replied. "Sit down and wait. Mr. Kinsley will be with you in a minute."

Stacey flopped down in a chair on the other side of the room. She was almost certain that Jenny had gotten her in trouble because they were both interested in Derek. She took a deep breath, trying to compose herself.

Stacey knew she couldn't get away with acting temperamental in front of Mr. Kinsley.

She'd have to pour on the charm, wrap him around her little finger. Men were always vulnerable to her charms.

Why should the vice-principal be any different?

After a few more minutes, the door swung open and Mr. Kinsley appeared in the archway. He was a tall, red-haired man with accusing green eyes and a narrow face. His expression was severe, but Stacey didn't buckle. She figured she could charm her way out of anything.

"I'll see you now, Miss Linden," the vice-principal said.

Stacey smiled. "Yes, sir."

She entered his office, which was dim and intimidating. She figured he kept it shady for effect. Mr. Kinsley was in charge of discipline for the school, so he was always having to dress down anyone who had gotten out of line. But Stacey wasn't afraid, at least not right away.

Stacey sat down in a chair opposite Mr. Kinsley's big oaken desk. She kept smiling, sure that she could wiggle out of whatever was wrong. After all, she hadn't done anything to be sorry for.

Mr. Kinsley leaned back in a plush leather chair and folded his hands. "Miss Linden, it has been brought to my attention that you missed the scholastic evaluation test this morning."

She laughed in a nonchalant way. "Oh, yes, I was sick this morning. But I'm better now."

His green eyes focused on her and he wasn't happy. "Miss Linden, your records show that you have never taken a scholastic evaluation exam since you arrived at Central."

Stacey still did not react to his scare tactics. "I'm just unlucky I guess. I can make it up any time. Maybe next week."

Kinsley pulled a test booklet from a drawer in his desk. "You're going to take the exam right now, Miss Linden."

"But I can't, I mean, I have classes," Stacey tried, figuring the excuse would work.

Kinsley dropped the test booklet on his desktop. "I'll see to it that you're excused from the rest of your classes for the day."

"I'd really rather not take it right now," Stacey replied. "I was sick to my stomach this morning, so my mom kept me home. I still feel a little weak."

Kinsley leaned forward, glaring at her. "Miss Linden, either you take the test right now, or I call your parents."

"But—"

"This is not negotiable," Kinsley went on. "You must complete this exam or I'll be forced to suspend you from classes at Central until you do."

A suspension! That would really wreck her social life. If she got suspended, her mother wouldn't let her date anymore. She'd probably take away Stacey's car too.

Kinsley picked up the phone. "Very well, if you don't want to take the exam, I'll have to call your father right now. Doesn't he work for the planning commission?"

"No! I mean, yes," Stacey replied, "he does work for the town but I don't think he's in his office today."

She was stretching, trying to buy time, stalling until she could think of a good excuse. She had to get out of this. Stacey hated taking exams.

Kinsley wasn't buying the dodge. "Well, we'll see if he's in his office today. I have the number right here."

"No!"

Kinsley put down the phone. "Then you want to take the test right now?"

Stacey touched her stomach. "I'm starting to feel a little sick, Mr. Kinsley."

"You felt well enough to come to school *after* the test was over," he challenged.

"Yes, but—"

He picked up the phone again. "If you're not feeling well, I'd better call your mother. Doesn't she work for the Parks and Recreation Department?"

"No, I mean—"

Kinsley hesitated with the phone in his hand.

"You have two choices, Miss Linden. You take the test or I call your parents."

It was Jenny, Stacey thought, it had to be. She had told Mr. Kinsley about Stacey missing the test. It was all Jenny's fault.

"What will it be, Stacey?" Harlan Kinsley asked.

Stacey sighed. "All right, I'll take the test."

She couldn't let her parents find out what she had been doing at school.

But as it turned out, the vice-principal had to call her mother and father even after Stacey had completed the exam.

FOUR

Mr. Kinsley leaned forward on his desk, his hands folded and a concerned expression on his thin face. "Thank you for coming, Mr. and Mrs. Linden. I know you're both busy, but when you hear what I have to say, I think you'll see the importance of this meeting."

Joseph Linden sat next to his wife, holding her hand. He was a tall, handsome, brown-haired man with deep blue eyes like his daughter. He wore a black business suit, a starched white shirt and a red tie. Stacey sat on the right side of her father, frowning like the whole thing was a crushing bore. But she was only hiding her fears that she had been caught in her little game. Now that her parents had been called into the vice-principal's office, the consequences would not be good.

Mr. Kinsley lifted a piece of paper, reading the results of Stacey's scholastic evaluation test. "These figures are fairly disturbing for a junior at Central Academy," he went on. "Stacey scored two hundred and five points out of a possible seven hundred and fifty. That's the lowest score I've seen since I've been here at Central."

A frown covered Mr. Linden's rugged face. "Could there be some mistake on the scoring? I mean, aren't these tests graded by a machine?"

Mr. Kinsley shook his head. "No, not this time. I graded Stacey's test myself. I even went over it a second time to make sure I hadn't made a mistake."

Mrs. Linden shifted in her chair. "Two hundred and five? That's impossible. Stacey's always been a good student."

Kinsley sighed. "Her grades would seem to bear that out, Mrs. Linden, but I'm afraid your daughter has been avoiding these scholastic evaluation tests since she came to Central. She hasn't taken one exam."

Mr. Linden turned to his daughter. "Is that true, Stacey?"

Stacey grimaced, folding her arms, sighing, not offering a reply to her father's question.

Mrs. Linden had an angry expression on her face. "You lied to me, Stacey. You said the school was having a senior assembly on the day of the test. Didn't you?"

Stacey's face was now beet-red. Even her ears felt hot. She had finally been caught in one of her ruses. And she hated it.

Mr. Kinsley referred to the test scores again. "According to this, Stacey is reading on a sixth-grade level. Her math scores are even lower. She didn't even bother to complete the history or social studies sections. And her English score in grammar and structure is barely on a sixth-grade level."

"How can this be?" her father asked. "She's always been a B student. Haven't you, Princess?"

Stacey sighed, not sure what to say. They had her dead to rights. How could she defend herself in light of the facts?

Mr. Kinsley's stern countenance focused on her. "Stacey, do you have an explanation for your father?"

"This is bogus," Stacey replied curtly. "I don't need some stupid exam to tell me I'm not smart. I always do my homework."

"Millie Johnson might disagree with you," Mr. Kinsley said. "Do you know Millie Johnson, Stacey?"

Stacey looked away. Had another person betrayed her? How could everything be falling down around her after she had been so careful all these years?

"Who is this Millie Johnson?" Mr. Linden asked.

"She's a girl who Stacey pays to do her homework," Mr. Kinsley replied. "I've been asking around about Stacey. It seems she pays several good students to regularly complete her assignments."

"But what about exams?" Mrs. Linden asked. "She can't get other students to take her tests for her."

Kinsley leveled his gaze on Stacey again. "My guess is that she cheats."

Mr. Linden almost came out of his chair. "Now just one minute! I won't have you accusing my daughter of cheating. You don't cheat, do you, Princess?"

Stacey turned toward her father. She was going to defend herself, but when she saw his caring expression, the emotions welled inside her. Tears pooled in her deep blue eyes. She put her face in her hands and started to cry.

Mr. Linden was incredibly disappointed. "Stacey, how could you? After your mother and I trusted you?"

Mrs. Linden had grown livid. "So that's it! You treat us like a couple of fools."

"No," Stacey sobbed. "It isn't like that. You don't understand, Mom. I—"

"Don't understand?" Mrs. Linden cried. "Cheating, getting other students to do your homework for you while you run around all over town like some tart. I understand perfectly! As of now, young lady, you can kiss your little green car good-bye."

"No!" Stacey whined. "Please—"

"We had plans for you," her mother went on.

"We've been saving so you could go to an Ivy League college. And this is how you repay our trust!"

Mr. Linden had also become irritated with his daughter. "Stacey, we believed in you. We wanted you to go to a good university."

"But I don't want to go to college," Stacey replied tearfully. "I want to be a model."

"Oh, that's right," Mrs. Linden rejoined. "We give you all the advantages so you can act like some dumb mannequin. That's rich, Stacey. Thanks a lot."

A tense silence descended on the meeting. Mrs. Linden was boiling. Stacey's father also seethed with anger. Stacey had embarrassed them horribly in front of Mr. Kinsley.

The vice-principal tried to calm them down. "This isn't the end of the world."

Mrs. Linden glared at Kinsley. "What do you suggest we do then? If she's reading on a sixth-grade level—"

"Your daughter isn't stupid," Kinsley replied quickly. "She's very bright in fact."

"But the test scores," Mr. Linden said. "Aren't they—"

"They aren't everything," Kinsley replied. "Granted, they do show some academic problems with Stacey, but I have to wonder if Stacey tries as hard as she could."

"Well?" Mrs. Linden challenged. "*Did* you try hard or did you ignore it like everything else?"

"I tried," Stacey said. "I really tried."

Mr. Kinsley leaned back, putting a hand to his chin. "Well, I think we may have another problem here."

Both of Stacey's parents looked up at the same time.

Mr. Linden's brow wrinkled. "What kind of problem?"

"Yes, what kind of problem?" her mother echoed.

"It's possible that Stacey has a learning disability."

Mr. Linden's face was suddenly full of hope. "A learning disability? Can't that be treated?"

"Well, there are certain techniques that are available to students with learning disabilities," Mr. Kinsley offered.

"Then we'll get the best possible treatment right away," her father offered. "I'll hire an expert if I have to."

"Are you sure she has a disability?" Mrs. Linden asked.

Kinsley shook his head. "No, I'm not a hundred percent certain. But we can have her evaluated. In fact, there's an ongoing program right here at Central."

Mr. Linden said, "Then get her into the program right away. I don't care what it costs."

Kinsley nodded. "All right."

Stacey, who had stopped crying, looked up at the vice-principal. "What kind of program is it?"

"It's part of a city adult education class," Mr. Kinsley replied. "Have you ever heard of Chandler Carr, Mr. Linden?"

"Uh, no, I don't believe I have," Stacey's father replied.

"I've heard of him," Mrs. Linden put in. "He's supposed to be an expert in adult education, part of the community outreach program."

"Precisely," Kinsley replied. "We were lucky to get him. He's a very busy man. The class is offered only at night."

Stacey grimaced. "At night?"

"Yes," the vice-principal replied. "Mr. Carr teaches two classes on Tuesday and Thursday nights."

"Would there be any problem getting Stacey into the class right away?" Mr. Linden asked.

Kinsley shrugged. "No, I don't think so. The adult education classes are just part of what Carr does at night. He can take Stacey as a special case, evaluate her and then prescribe what she needs to bring her academic skills up to par."

"Let's do it then," Mrs. Linden rejoined. "The sooner the better. I want her in those classes now."

Stacey shook her head, glaring at them. "Wait a minute. There's no way that I'm taking night classes."

"You'll do as you're told, young lady," her mother replied. "You don't have any say in this."

"Night classes?" Stacey said again. "But, that's for geeks and dweebs."

Mr. Linden tried to be more understanding. "It won't be so bad, Princess. Besides, you need it if you're going on to college."

"I'm not going to college!" Stacey cried. "I'm going to New York to be a model!"

"Even models need high school educations," Kinsley offered. "And your father is right, Stacey. It won't be that bad."

Stacey shook her head. "No way. I'm not ruining my life with night classes."

"As of now, you don't *have* a life," her mother said. "There'll be no more dating. No more nights out, especially on school nights."

"I'm not going to night school!" Stacey insisted.

Mr. Kinsley took a deep breath. "Stacey, if you don't enter this program, I'm afraid I'll have to suspend you from classes. I might even have to expel you from Central altogether."

"I don't care," Stacey said. "I'm not going to take night classes!"

"That's enough, young lady!"

Stacey stiffened. The bellowing had come from her father. He was glaring at her with an angry intensity that she had seen very few times in her life. He was serious now, not the doting father who called her *Princess*.

"But, Dad—"

"No *buts*," Joseph Linden replied. "You've

been getting away with murder and now it's going to stop."

"I'll run away from home!" Stacey threatened. "I'll quit school. I swear I will."

Her father pointed a finger at her. "Go ahead. Run away. Quit school. But as long as you're under our roof, you're going to do what we say, young lady. Is that understood?"

Stacey broke down again, crying. Her bluff's hadn't worked. Her mother and father couldn't be fooled anymore.

Like it or not, Stacey was going to night class.

FIVE

Stacey lay on the pink and white comforter of her bed, staring at the ceiling of the dark room. For nearly a week, she had been grounded, forced to stay home every night. No dates, no shopping, nothing but school and her studies. It was torture for her. In Stacey's mind, life as she knew it was over.

She was a little scared too. For the first time in her young life, Stacey felt that she was not in control. She had always been the manipulator, the instigator. But now her fate seemed to be out of her hands.

Some of her fears stemmed from the actual school work itself. Stacey had thought that she *could* do the lessons assigned by her teachers at Central Academy. But she had simply chosen *not* to study because she could get by with her cheating. Now that she had been forced to crack the books, Stacey felt lost, insecure, inadequate. Studying was a lot harder than she imagined. Was she really stupid? Or did she have that learning disability that Mr. Kinsley had talked about?

Stacey would soon find out the truth. It was Tuesday, the first night of classes. Night class—dweebarama!

She would have started crying, except that the phone rang next to her bed. "Hello?"

"Hi, babe, it's me, Derek."

Stacey sighed. "Oh."

"Hey, what's wrong?" Derek asked. "You sound like it's the end of the world."

"I'm grounded," Stacey replied.

Derek laughed. "Get real."

"No, I'm serious. I got in all this trouble in school. Big trouble with my mom and dad too."

Derek gave a mocking groan. "Stacey, you don't get *into* trouble, you *cause* it."

She laughed weakly at his joke. It was good to hear from Derek—from anyone. The phone hadn't rung in over a week.

"What's up with you?" she asked. "I thought we were through. I haven't seen you at all."

He sighed. "I'm sorry about that, babe. It's just—well, I hate to admit it, but you get to me. I really care about you, Stace. I really do."

"Aw, that's sweet," she replied, feeling some of the old confidence returning. "I've missed you."

He sounded hopeful. "Yeah?"

But she didn't want him to get too cocky. "You haven't called me in ages, Derek. That stinks."

"Aw, come on, sweet thing. Don't be like that."

Stacey smiled. "Be like what?"

Derek tried to change the subject. "Hey, what do you say? Me and you out tonight. There's a great band at the Road House. I think I can get us in. It's a slow night and my buddy is working the door. He won't ask for I.D."

Stacey exhaled, gazing at the ceiling again. "I can't, Derek. Not tonight."

"Oh. I see. You're still mad at me. Okay. Well, listen, I'm sorry I bothered you—"

"No, it's not like that. I—I have something else to do."

"That college guy," Derek accused. "It's him, isn't it? I'm not good enough for you because I'm only a high school kid."

"No, it's not that," Stacey replied. "I told you, I'm grounded by my parents."

"You said you had something else to do, Stacey. Don't lie to me. I'm not stupid, you know."

She sat up on her bed, afraid that she might lose him if she didn't tell him the truth. "Derek, it's not what you think." Suddenly, she realized that she cared about him, that he was important to her.

"No? Well, I think you're playing your old games."

"Derek, listen to me. Oh, this is so embarrassing. But I'm going to tell you the truth."

"That'll be a first."

"No, just listen." She took a deep breath. "Derek, I have to go to school tonight."

"Aw, come on, Stace, you can do better than that!"

"No, I mean it, Derek, I have to go to night class. It's part of my punishment. My mom and dad are making me."

"Brutal," Derek replied.

"I know, I know. It's horrible."

"Hey, babe, you never let anything like this stop you before. You can handle it, can't you?"

Stacey hesitated. "Well, I—I guess I could."

"Sure," Derek went on. "Who's teaching this stupid class anyway? Some dweeb?"

"A guy named Carr," she replied. "Chandler Carr. He only teaches night classes."

"No wonder I never heard of him. But, hey, that's a dweeb name. And you can work your magic, Stacey. He won't have a chance against your blue eyes."

Stacey sighed. "I don't know, Derek. My mom and dad are on top of this one. They expect results."

"So you deal with it," Derek told her. "Hey, I never knew my Stacey to lie down and die. You can't give up, babe. Ditch the class and meet me at the club. Okay?"

Stacey's body stiffened with a new resolve. "Yeah, why not? They can't push me around. I think there's a break during the class. I'll make an appearance and then blow off the whole thing."

"Now you're talking. See ya at the club."

Stacey hung up, smiling. She felt like her old self now. They couldn't stop her from doing what she wanted. She'd get out of the night class the same way she had dealt with everything else at Central Academy.

"Stacey, are you ready?"

She looked up to see her mother at the doorway of her bedroom.

"Uh, I still have to change clothes," Stacey told her.

Mrs. Linden glanced at her watch. "I'm afraid you don't have time. We have to leave right away if you're going to make it to the class on time."

Stacey grimaced. "Mom!"

Mrs. Linden put her hands on her hips. "Now listen to me, young lady. You're not going to get away with that attitude anymore. *You* violated the spirit of our agreement by cheating—"

"No, I—"

"—so all bets are off. Now you better be ready to go in two minutes. I'm driving you to Central."

Stacey's jaw dropped. "You?"

"You don't think I'm going to trust you after what you've pulled in the past, do you?"

"But I—"

"And I'm picking you up after class, is that understood?"

Stacey glanced at the floor, pouting, refusing to answer.

"Stacey?"

"All right!"

"Two minutes," Mrs. Linden commanded. "And I mean it!"

It wasn't fair, Stacey thought. She didn't deserve such horrid treatment. And she surely didn't merit a terrible fate like going to night class.

Mrs. Linden dropped Stacey at the front entrance of the Central campus, leaving her with a warning that Stacey had better put forth her best effort. Stacey walked away from the car without a word. Her face flushed with anger as she stormed up the front steps.

The campus seemed strange at night. Stacey realized that she had never been to Central after dark. Her anger quickly turned into a feeling of curiosity and then dread. What was she doing here at school, wasting a whole evening?

As Stacey walked slowly down the dim corridor of the senior classroom building, she started to formulate a scheme in her mind. Derek was right—she could wrap any guy around her little finger, especially some dweeb named Chandler Carr.

What could he be anyway? Nothing but a geek. Probably had thick glasses and a pocket protector for all his pens and pencils. She'd lay a story on him, duck out, hang with Derek, and then dart back to school to meet her mother in front of the campus. No prob.

But first she had to find the classroom. Stacey had never been to classes in the senior building. She had walked with a few of her boyfriends in the hallways, but she really didn't know her way around.

Reaching into the pocket of her jeans, she took out the piece of paper that had been given to her by Mr. Kinsley. "Room three-oh-two," she said to no one.

Glancing up, Stacey suddenly realized that she was all alone in the hallway. Where was everyone? Wasn't this supposed to be a whole class full of people? Her eyes lifted to the number above the first door to her left.

It was room one-ninety-nine. She started walking again, ambling down the corridor as the room numbers grew larger. The halls were awfully quiet at night—too quiet. Stacey felt a chill in her shoulders.

"This is crazy," she muttered to herself.

Were those footsteps behind her, shuffling on the floor?

Turning quickly, she stole a look into the shadows, expecting to see someone.

Was that a male figure turning the corner, going away from her?

"Hello?" she called in a meek voice.

No reply from the dim recesses of the senior building.

"I'll never forgive them," Stacey said, cursing her mother and father for dooming her to such a fate.

As she started to turn around again, a dark shape loomed in front of her. Stacey cried out and took a step backward. Suddenly there was a man standing in her way. He wore a dumb look on his face. He was a lot older than Stacey.

"Uh, didn't mean to scare you," he said in a dull tone. "I was lookin' for room three-oh-two. My name is Elvin."

Stacey took a deep breath, trembling, trying to compose herself. "Get away from me."

A hurt expression crossed the man's slack face. "Uh, I said I was sorry. I just need to find room three-oh-two."

It dawned on Stacey that this churlish character was going to be in her class. He was dressed in baggy work clothes that smelled of sweat. It was going to be even more horrible than she imagined.

"Three-oh-two?" he asked again.

"Uh, I'm looking for it, too," Stacey replied, bolting around him. "I think it's up this way."

Stacey began to stride rapidly away from him. She quickly outdistanced the man who had a lumbering walk. In a few minutes, she was standing in front of room three-oh-two.

"I can't do this," she muttered. "They can't make me. I'll quit school. I—"

But she knew that her threats were in vain. Where would she go if she left her parents? She wasn't ready for New York, not yet. She didn't have any money. And she knew her parents wouldn't let her take the car if she left. Stacey was trapped.

When she opened the door, twenty-five or thirty pairs of curious eyes looked at her. The people were older, some of them even had graying hair.

They were worse than geeks—they were adults.

Stacey started to turn back but the lumbering Elvin staggered into the doorway, blocking her retreat.

"Hey, ya found it," he said. "Good goin'."

Stacey moved out of his way, allowing Elvin to walk past her. He took a seat in the front row. Stacey just stood there, unable to stay or go. If only their eyes weren't rivetted on her.

"Are you the teacher?" someone asked.

"Nah," another voice rejoined, "she's too young. Look at her."

"Our teacher's a man," another one said.

"Pity," said some geeky man.

The entire class laughed out loud.

Stacey was mortified. Where had these creatures come from? Her mom had said that the night class was part of some community outreach program, but Stacey had never seen *these* people in her community. They had come out of some freak show.

"Why don't you sit down?" Elvin asked.

Stacey wanted to run. But she had to stay, at least until the teacher came. She didn't want to be in any more trouble. She just wanted her old life back.

She stepped toward one of the desks, keeping her deep blue eyes aimed at the floor. She did not want to look at them. They were a different species, inhuman creatures to be avoided at all costs.

Taking a desk behind Elvin, she sat down, wondering how she was going to get out of this. She could never be a night class dweeb. Her parents would just have to understand. If they wanted to get help for her, they could hire a private tutor. Anything was better than being locked up with this bunch of neanderthals.

Suddenly, Elvin whirled around and smiled at her. "This is my first night. I didn't bring any paper or pencils. Can I borrow some of yours?"

"I—I don't have any," Stacey replied.

She had forgotten to bring her notebook. But she had a locker in the junior building. She could run over there to get them.

Stacey tried to smile at Elvin. "Uh, I have to go to my locker. If the teacher shows up, tell him I'll be right back. Can you do that for me, Elvin?"

"Sure. Will you let me borrow some paper and a pencil?" he asked dumbly.

"Whatever you say, Elvin."

Stacey jumped out of the desk and bolted from the classroom. She ran through the hall, exiting at the far end, rushing across the plaza to the junior building. The night was misty and cool, a typical autumn evening for Port City. There seemed to be other classes going on in the junior building. The hall doors were open, allowing Stacey access to her locker. She grabbed her notebook and ran back to the senior building. But when she arrived at the door of room three-oh-two, she couldn't make herself go inside.

"They have to let me out of this," she said as she stood petrified in front of the doorway. "I can't, I just can't."

Stacey started to turn and run again.

But this time, a strong hand closed around her wrist.

"No!" Stacey cried. "Let go."

She tried to struggle but the grip was too strong.

Stacey felt someone drawing her closer.

She glanced up, gasping for breath.

Suddenly she was looking into a pair of the darkest eyes she had ever seen.

SIX

Stacey was frozen by the hypnotic intensity of the man's incredibly dark eyes. The irises were dark blue—no, almost black. Ebony circles stared back at her from an incredibly handsome face. He was holding on to her wrist, but Stacey did not try to get away. She just stood there, peering into those dark eyes, eyes even a deeper blue than her own.

His full, reddish lips parted slightly. "Good evening," he said in a rich voice.

Stacey nodded. She couldn't think of anything to say. A chill seemed to spread from his hand through her entire body.

"Were you going somewhere?" the dark-eyed man asked in a polite tone.

"Uh—I—I don't know," Stacey heard herself say.

The man smiled broadly. "Have you lost your way?"

Stacey shook her head. His grip was strong

on her wrist, yet she no longer felt a compulsion
to draw back. Though she had never seen this
stranger before, she seemed to instinctively
trust him. And those shining eyes were unbe-
lievably dark and bright at the same time.

Suddenly he let go of her. "I'm sorry," he said.
"That's very forward of me. I shouldn't have
grabbed you like that. It's just—" He hesitated
for a moment, not finishing the sentence.

Stacey smiled. "It's all right."

They were silent for a moment. Stacey noticed that he had shoulder-length black hair
that rode the seams of a pale linen coat. Black
shirt, no tie, matching linen pants. His complexion was as white as the linen suit. He was
handsome with a aristocratic nose and perfect
teeth, one of the best looking men that Stacey
had ever seen in her life.

"Are you Stacey Linden?" he asked without
warning.

Stacey blushed. "Why, yes, I—"

How did he know her name?

"Are you here for the night class?"

She nodded. "Are you taking the class too?"
She hoped this hunky guy would sit next to her.

He laughed slightly. "No, I'm teaching the
class. And we'd better get in there before my
students get restless." He took her arm and
started to lead her toward the classroom.

"*Teaching* the class?" Stacey asked.

"Yes, I'm Chandler Carr."

How could a guy this young be teaching the class? He didn't look much older than the college guy she had been dating. Chandler Carr was certainly no older than twenty-one.

The adult students were laughing and talking when Stacey entered the classroom on the arm of Chandler Carr. There was some whispering as Stacey sat down at her desk behind Elvin. But Stacey was no longer embarrassed. She didn't even seem to notice them. She couldn't take her eyes off the impressive figure of Chandler Carr.

Chandler stood behind his desk, not saying a word for a few moments. The class gradually piped down, turning to focus on the teacher. Stacey glanced up to see that he was looking right at her, smiling. Reflexively, she smiled back, not sure what she was feeling toward this classy gentleman.

"We have a new student," Chandler said to the class. "Her name is Stacey Linden. Now, she isn't seeking an adult diploma like most of you, but she's here for a special evaluation."

Elvin, who was grinning broadly, spoke up. "I wouldn't mind givin' her some special evaluation."

The class laughed, at least until they noticed the expression on the instructor's face. Chandler Carr had grown sullen. His white face had tightened into an accusing scowl.

Elvin kept guffawing, glancing back at an

embarrassed Stacey. Chandler Carr came around the desk, walking toward Elvin. He was almost on the tall, gawky man when Elvin turned to notice him.

"Whatta you want?" Elvin asked in a hostile tone.

Chandler Carr just stared at the brute. Stacey was suddenly afraid. Chandler wasn't big like Elvin. He had a slight build, slim and delicate looking. Elvin could probably stomp him in a scuffle—or at least that was the way it looked.

"I don't believe I recognize you," Carr said in a calm voice.

Elvin laughed. "My buddy told me about this class. Thought I'd try it out and see what it's about."

But Chandler did not seem to share Elvin's sense of humor. "You can't just walk in here without registering with the proper authorities."

Elvin swung his head in a semi-circle, appealing to the class, all of whom were watching intently. "Naw, I don't have to do nothin' like that, do I?"

No reply from the class. They were all starting to worry, like Stacey. Would there be a fight? Would the huge Elvin break Chandler Carr into several pieces?

Chandler remained silent, staring at Elvin. The big man gradually looked up into the dark eyes that had so enraptured Stacey. Stacey saw Elvin shudder when he met the teacher's steely gaze.

"You don't belong in this class," Chandler said calmly.

Elvin was dumbfounded. His mouth hung open. All the hostile confidence had gone out of him.

"You don't belong in this class," the instructor repeated.

"I don't belong in this class," Elvin responded, sounding far away.

"And you're going to leave right now."

Elvin said. "I'm going to leave right now."

"You're going to get up and walk through the door and you're not coming back until you've registered with the proper authorities," Chandler went on.

"I'm walking through the door," Elvin replied. "Not comin' back till I registered with the proper 'thorities."

"Good evening."

Elvin rose from his desk and made a slow exit, closing the door behind him.

As soon as he was gone, the classroom erupted in applause.

"Way to go, Mr. Carr."

"Wow, that was cool."

"How'd he do it?"

Chandler made his way to the desk, taking a slight, mocking bow. "A dubious candidate for

higher education. But now, back to the business
at hand. As I said before, this lovely young
lady—"

He had called her lovely! Stacey felt her heart
throbbing. She had never experienced such a
sensation, at least not for a guy. It was similar
to the rush that Stacey got from downhill skiing
in the winter.

"—is here for special evaluation. But as for
the rest of you, I see some more new faces out
there, which is all right. As you know, this is an
ongoing program. So if you'll hand me your
registration papers right now—"

Stacey could not take her gaze off him as he
moved lithely around the classroom picking up
the registration forms. Could this be love at
first sight? No—lightning had never struck her
like this before. It had to be something else.
Why couldn't she stop staring at him?

As soon as he had gathered the papers, Chandler stepped up next to Stacey's desk, smiling at
her. "I'll get them started on tonight's lesson and
then we can talk."

Stacey nodded, feeling flushed all over. Why
did he have this effect on her? There was
something extraordinary in his looks, his manner, his charisma. But she couldn't be falling for
him already—he was her teacher, for starters.

His voice filled the classroom, charming the
class. Most of the other students were adults
who, for some reason or other, had not com-

pleted their high school education. Chandler Carr was there to make sure they did so now.

He assigned the new students the task of writing a short paragraph on why they wanted a high school diploma. The others had to get started in whatever workbook was required for the individual subjects needed to complete their course requirements.

When everyone else was hard at work, Chandler came toward Stacey, smiling again. Those black eyes were flashing now, sometimes changing to deep blue. He held a test booklet in his hand.

"I hate to give you a test on your first night," he said to Stacey, "but otherwise I have no way to evaluate your skills. I believe Mr. Kinsley thinks you have a learning disability, but since I'm the expert, I'll have to make that determination for myself."

Stacey just nodded, feeling like a lump of Jell-O. No human being had ever touched her so deeply, so quickly. She had experienced crushes on rock stars and a few other guys, but this was something she didn't understand. She had only known Chandler for a few minutes, but the feeling seemed to go beyond infatuation.

"Just do your best on the exam," he told her, "and don't worry, you won't be graded, at least not by conventional standards. But I have to know certain things about your academic standing before I can help you."

"Yes, Mr. Carr," she said dutifully.

He laughed a little. "You can call me Chandler."

"Chandler," she repeated.

He winked at her. "Don't tell Mr. Kinsley that you call me by my first name. He can be a little, well, tight, if you know what I mean."

She grinned. "I know."

"Do you have a number-two pencil?"

"Yes," Stacey replied.

He patted her shoulder, thrilling her to the marrow. "Just concentrate and do your best."

"I will," she said. "I really will."

Chandler moved away, gliding over the floor with an effortless gait. He was so handsome, so smooth. His shoulder-length hair glistened under the ceiling lights. Was he too old for Stacey? No, he couldn't be more than four or five years her senior. And he was mature, confident, not like the teenaged boys she had been dating.

Stacey reached into her notebook, taking out a number-two pencil, the same pencil she had used on her scholastic evaluation test. She opened the test booklet, gazing down at the first question. For a second, she experienced the same old feeling of revulsion that had always come with school. But then she glanced up to see Chandler Carr smiling at her. When she lowered her eyes to the page, Stacey had a new sense of concentration.

Suddenly, Stacey didn't mind night school at all.

"Stacey, are you finished?"

She looked up from the test paper, gazing into Chandler's eyes. "Uh, yes, I just answered the last question."

"I'll take your paper," he told her.

Stacey handed him the test booklet, smiling. "So, what do we do now?" She noticed that the classroom was empty.

"Class is over," he replied. "Everyone else is gone for the evening. You should be leaving as well."

Stacey frowned. She didn't want the class to be over. She wanted to stay and listen to Chandler's soothing voice.

"Can't I wait while you grade my paper?" she asked.

He smiled and laughed a little. "I'm afraid it doesn't work like that, Stacey. I have to compile your results. It could take several days. And, as I said before, you won't be graded as such, but you will be evaluated."

"Oh." She sat there for a moment, not sure what to do. "Uh, then that's it?"

He nodded. "I hope it wasn't too arduous for you," Chandler offered in a kind tone. "Night classes can be—"

"Oh, no! I mean, I'm a night person."

"Really?" he said. "So am I. I always hated my early classes when I was in college."

"Yeah, morning classes are a bummer," Stacey replied. She winced. Had she really said *bummer*? An intelligent guy like Chandler wouldn't use such a word.

"Are you going to college?" he asked.

Stacey shrugged. "No, I want to be a model."

"You should consider college," he went on. "You know, Cindy Crawford studied chemical engineering."

"Really?"

He nodded reassuringly. "The age of the 'dumb model' is over, Stacey. Even if you're going to survive on your looks, you still have to develop your mind."

He was drawing her in, exciting her.

"I never thought of it like that," Stacey said.

He smiled, warm and charming. "You have a good evening, now. And I'll see you on Thursday. I'll have your test results by then."

"Okay."

He turned away from her, walking toward the desk.

Stacey rose slowly, still watching him. Where had he come from? What was he like outside the classroom? She found herself wanting to know every detail of his life.

Hesitating at the door, she glanced back toward Chandler. He lifted his head to meet her gaze. The electricity, the chemistry was incredible.

"Yes?" he asked.

Stacey blushed. "Uh, I just wanted to say, well—just—thanks. For helping me."

"That's my job," he replied, looking away.

His job?

Stacey was mortified at Chandler Carr's nonchalance. Hadn't *she* felt the connection between them? So *he* had to feel it too. Didn't he? Or was it one-sided on her part?

Stacey had always driven boys wild. Now she had a crush on someone who had suddenly grown cold. Was this what it felt like to be ignored? A gnawing, uneasy sensation rattled her nerves and her stomach.

Chandler seemed to sense her presence, because he spoke to her without turning around. "Was there something else?"

"No. I mean, see ya."

Stacey fled into the hallway, feeling like a total dweeb. Had she made a fool of herself in front of Chandler Carr? He probably thought she was some kind of blushing schoolgirl with a crush—which she was!

Leaning back against the wall, Stacey closed her eyes, trying not to think about Chandler's incredible charisma. She *couldn't* fall for a teacher. He was older than her and it had to be against school policy.

But Chandler was such a babe! No, she had to

put it out of her mind. She was in night school to better herself. If only he didn't have those haunting black eyes that pierced her soul.

"No way," she told herself. "Forget it."

Stacey started slowly down the hallway. She knew her mother would be waiting outside. What a slap in the face! Her mother hadn't taken her to school since the sixth grade.

Still, things were looking up, she thought as she passed the rows of lockers. She *had* completed the first night class. That would surely make her parents happy. Even better, she had changed her mind about night class. The teacher had brought her around. Maybe it wasn't going to be so bad after all.

Stacey heard something shuffling behind her. Slow footsteps. Chandler had come after her. He wanted to talk. He wanted to say that he was also attracted to her.

She turned toward the steps. "Chandler—"

But it wasn't her handsome instructor.

Instead, a thick, rough hand closed over her mouth.

She struggled, but she wasn't strong enough.

A pair of brutish arms pinned her against the wall of lockers. She felt a heavy weight pressing against her body.

SEVEN

Elvin, the hulking brute Chandler had ejected from class, had grabbed her in the hallway. His face came close to hers. Stacey could smell the stench of beer on his breath.

"You!" he said in a raspy whisper. "You and that teacher of yours made me a fool in front of the class."

Stacey wanted to shake her head, but he was too strong. There was no escape.

"Smarty pants," he slurred. "That's what you are. Always hated the smarty pants kind. Made me leave school in the first place. Smarty pants, you gotta pay."

Pay how? Stacey wondered frantically.

His eyes were narrow slits as he peered into her frightened face. "You're pretty. Popular too, I bet. You a cheerleader?"

She tried to shake her head again.

"I bet you're a cheerleader. Always make the

pretty ones cheerleaders. Date the big quarter-back!"

A muffled "No" was lost between his fingers.

"I played football," he growled. "But I was too dumb to pass so I quit. Just quit. What do you think about that, Miss Popular?"

He wouldn't have heard her reply, she knew, even if she had been able to give one.

An ugly smile crossed his lips. "We're gonna have some fun. Yeah, just you and me. And you ain't gonna tell nobody, 'cause if you do, I'm gonna kill you!"

Stacey sank her teeth into his fingers. The drunken behemoth didn't seem to notice the pain.

"Where we gonna have fun, Miss Popular? Huh? It's you and me. A date for the senior prom."

Stacey tried to scream, her cries suppressed by his thick hand. How would she get away from him? He was too big and mean for her to inflict any serious damage on him. And there certainly wasn't any way to reason with him.

"How 'bout right here?" Elvin asked in an angry whisper. "You and me. A dance for the prom. You wanna dance?"

Stacey didn't venture a reply.

"Dance, dance, dance," he went on. "You and me, king and queen of the prom."

Stacey's body trembled. Her knees were weak. She had never been in a spot like this.

But there didn't seem to be any escape route. She could barely draw breath from the cool night air.

"How's about a kiss, sweety doll? Come on, give your Elvin a little—"

A cry of pain resounded from his throat. Suddenly he let go of her. Stacey slumped back against the locker, not sure why he had released his grip.

"Let go of me!" the brute bellowed, his desperate voice echoing in the corridor.

Another voice joined the bestial cry. "You lout! How dare you accost this young woman!"

It was Chandler Carr. Stacey saw him now. He had grabbed Elvin's shoulder. For the moment, he had rescued her, but Stacey feared that the hulking intruder might hurt him.

Sure enough, Elvin tried to wheel around to throw a punch at the smaller man. Chandler ducked the blow easily. Suddenly, Elvin's body was flying through the air, crashing against the lockers. His huge frame slumped to the floor, as if he had been bested by super-human strength. When Elvin tried to get up, Chandler kicked him in the face, sending the brute into an unconscious state.

Stacey could not believe her eyes. Had Chandler really taken out this hostile giant? He moved in front of her, peering at her intensely.

"Are you all right?" he asked.

Stacey was on the verge of tears. "He came at me—"

Chandler took her hand. "It's all right. Look at me."

She found herself drifting in his gaze. A calmness came over her almost instantly. It was as if the attack had never happened.

"You feel fine," Chandler told her.

"Yes, I feel fine," Stacey repeated.

He stroked her forehead with a gentle hand. "You don't remember him attacking you, do you?"

"No, I don't remember. I—Mr. Carr, hi!"

She smiled, under some sort of spell that he had cast on her.

"I'll walk you outside," Chandler Carr told her. "You'll be safe with me."

He held her hand to the end of the corridor, letting go when they exited through the front door.

Mrs. Linden was waiting in the car at the curb with the motor running. "Hello, Stacey." She looked at Chandler Carr with a dubious expression.

"Hello, Mrs. Linden," Chandler said. "I'm Stacey's teacher. I just wanted you to know that I'll have Stacey's test results by the next class."

Mrs. Linden smiled.Obviously taken in by his charms. "Well, if you're free before class Thursday, why don't you bring the test results and stay for dinner?"

Stacey smiled at her mother, which surprised Mrs. Linden, who had been expecting a groan at the invitation.

"That would be cool," Stacey said. "Please, Mr. Carr. Come."

"Uh, I don't know about dinner," Chandler replied. "I'm on a special diet. But I'd be happy to stop by with the results. And then I could drive Stacey to class—if that's all right with you, Mrs. Linden?"

"Of course," Stacey's mother replied. "We'd love to have you. Six o'clock?"

"Six-thirty, if that's all right," he replied. "It won't take long for me to give you the results. I'll be tied up until after dark, but I'll see you then."

Stacey grinned at him. "See you."

He smiled and turned away.

Stacey got into the car with her mother. "Hi, Mom."

Mrs. Linden squinted at her. "How was it?"

Stacey shrugged. "Fine. I really like Mr. Carr. He gave me a test. Only I won't be graded on it."

"I understand."

Stacey leaned back in the seat. "It was fun."

"What?" Mrs. Linden asked, dumbfounded.

"I said it was fun, Mom."

Mrs. Linden shook her head, not quite certain that she was hearing right. Her daughter seemed relaxed, confident. Stacey was a new girl after one evening session.

She hadn't expected her daughter to enjoy night school.

Thick white mist swirled before her. She was standing in her own backyard in Prescott Estates. Billows of fog rolled in from the direction of the Tide Gate River. But Stacey didn't seem to feel the chilly night air, even though she wore only a flimsy nightgown.

He was waiting for her. She could sense him in the dense fog. In a few moments, she saw his dark form moving through the ghostly white vapor.

"Chandler," she called to the fog. "Are you there?"

Something moved in the whirling cloud of moisture. A shape appeared before her. Only it wasn't human. Instead, a canine form ran toward her. It was a dog—no, a wolf.

But Stacey wasn't afraid of the wolf. She bent to pet him. The wolf licked her fingers.

The wolf wagged his tail, turning in circles like a house pet. Then he turned toward the fog, yelping for Stacey to follow. She ran across the wet grass, following the wolf. They were kindred spirits, recreating the night for themselves, unfettered by the constraints of daylight.

Stacey knelt beside her devoted friend, wrapping her arms around his thick neck. She hugged him like a warm puppy. The wolf licked her face, never once brushing her skin with the sharp teeth that could've ripped out her throat.

"Good boy!"

A foghorn sounded somewhere in the distance, pealing through the town. Stacey stood up quickly. She was compelled to peer in the direction of the horn.

When she glanced back, her pet was gone. In his place stood a man. She recognized the face immediately.

"Chandler!" she cried.

But when she tried to take a step toward him, he held out his hand. "No, Stacey. It can never be," he told her.

"But—"

"Return to your bed, Stacey. Don't think of me in that way. It can never be."

Tears welled in her eyes and her voice cracked. "But, I—I love you, Chandler."

"It can never be," he repeated.

She reached for him with outstretched arms as he receded into the fog, disappearing in a swirl of mist.

Stacey wanted to follow him but her legs were frozen. She could only watch as he abandoned her. Suddenly, she was unable to breathe. The mist was choking her. She squirmed and struggled until she awakened in her bed.

Stacey sat up, sweating. As soon as she opened her eyes, she forgot about the dream.

Still, the sensation of loss and despair lingered for a moment.

His name formed on her lips. "Chandler?"

But there was no reply.

Why had she called his name?

Had she been dreaming about him?

A cool wind stirred the papers on her desk and vanity. She saw that her window was open. Stacey climbed out of bed, hurrying to shut the casement.

Had the window been open when she went to sleep? She vaguely remembered coming home from night school, but that was all. Everything else seemed to be a blur.

She peered out at the fog that rolled lazily over the backyard. The skin of her face was damp. Her nightgown had also been moistened from the mist. But she hadn't been outside in the fog . . . or had she?

Stacey looked down at her feet, which were also wet. She had pieces of wet grass clinging to her skin. And there seemed to be some kind of markings on her gown. And fur—long, dark strands of animal hair, like she had been playing with a dog.

I must've been sleepwalking, she thought.

Stacey took a deep breath, gazing into the fog for a while longer. It was so thick, almost comforting. She felt as if she could fly forth into it, where someone waited.

"Chandler," she whispered to no one.

She thought of him standing before the class. He was so handsome and charming. Why did she experience such serenity, such contentment in his company? It had to be love.

A voice seemed to come out of the fog. "Sleep," it called in an eerie whisper.

Stacey's eyes grew wider. For a second, she thought she saw a dark shape gliding through the vapor. But then there was nothing beyond the dull blast of the foghorn.

Her eyes grew heavy. She returned to her bed, pulling the covers over her slender body. As soon as she closed her eyes, she slept dreamlessly until morning.

The next day at school, Stacey wandered the halls in a trance. She wasn't quite sure what had happened to her the night before. She only knew that she felt relaxed, serene. A peaceful disposition had claimed her entire being. Somehow, the calmness made the school day easier.

Stacey also found that it was easier to concentrate in her classes. Once, in history, she even raised her hand and gave the correct answer, much to the shock and delight of her teacher. And just how had she known the answer to the question, she wondered.

Maybe she had been listening all along when she was sitting in class. She hadn't cared before about learning. But she knew what, or *who*, had piqued her interest.

"Chandler."

The name formed on her lips like a secret wish. He was so—so everything. She couldn't stop thinking about him.

As she made for the cafeteria at lunchtime, Stacey entertained vain notions of Chandler and herself together. She saw them doing things together, kissing, holding hands. She hadn't felt like this since . . . well, ever.

But how could they possibly get together? He was older, a teacher. And why would he want someone like Stacey?

"Hey, babe, you stood me up last night!"

She lifted her eyes to see Derek Barton standing right in front of her. "Oh, hi."

She kept walking, moving around him. Derek fell in beside her. They strolled across the plaza on a brisk autumn afternoon.

"What happened?" he asked.

Stacey shrugged. "Night class, Derek. I can't get out of it. My parents are on top of me. Mom even drives me to school."

Derek sighed. "Tough. It was dead last night anyway. I left about eleven." Derek glanced sideways at her. "Did you hear the news this morning?"

"No," Stacey replied absently. "What?"

Derek shuddered. "I was there when they fished him out of the river. Some guy from Pitney Docks."

"What happened?" she asked, though she could not have cared less.

"I don't know. They said on the news he was a druggie. Had some needle marks in his arms."

She saw the cafeteria entrance ahead of them. "Too bad."

He said, "Yeah, I guess. I didn't know the dude, but I used to see him around town. He drank a lot but I never knew he was a junkie."

"Oh," she replied as she went through the archway, entering the cafeteria. "I'm sorry."

Derek stayed right behind her. "Yeah, his name was Elvin. He used to be kinda bad, but—"

Stacey stopped and grabbed his arm. "Elvin?"

"Yeah, did you know him too?"

Stacey's mind went blank. For an instant, the name had seemed familiar. But she couldn't recall ever having met the guy.

"No," she said softly. "I didn't know him."

They went through the serving line together. Derek kept talking about the way the cops had pulled the body onto the bank. A couple of employees on a waterfront restaurant had seen the corpse floating past them.

But Stacey didn't hear a word he said. She could not stop thinking of Chandler Carr. Her night class instructor would be coming to her house tomorrow. She would get to be with him again.

After dark.

EIGHT

Stacey stood by the window, gazing toward the street in front of her house. Outside, the shadows were deepening over Port City. Darkness would soon envelop the seacoast village, which meant the imminent arrival of Chandler Carr at the Linden residence. He would come with the night. Stacey had butterflies in her stomach, the anxiety of anticipation.

Stacey had abandoned any hopes of forgetting about Chandler. The attraction was too great. She had never experienced a feeling like this before. It was the strongest emotion that had ever surfaced in her heart.

She had to have him.

"Stacey?"

She glanced over her shoulder. Mrs. Linden stood at the archway of the living room. Stacey nodded to her mother and turned back toward the street.

"Are you nervous?" Mrs. Linden asked. "About your teacher coming here, I mean?"

Stacey shrugged, trying to mask her true feelings. "No, not really. It's okay."

Mrs. Linden squinted at her daughter. She had never seen Stacey like this. What had gotten into her?

"What do you know about this man?" her mother asked.

"He's really nice. I—"

"What man are you talking about, girls?"

Mr. Linden had come into the living room with his newspaper. He had been reading about the man who was pulled from the river. It was the big topic of conversation all over Port City.

"We were talking about Chandler Carr, Stacey's night class teacher," Mrs. Linden replied.

"Oh." Mr. Linden walked over to his easy chair and plopped down, opening the paper. "That stiff they found in the river. Not a drop of blood in him. He—"

Stacey glared at her father. "Dad!"

"What?"

"Don't talk like that around Chandler," Stacey said. "I don't want you to embarrass me."

Mr. Linden leaned forward. "Why is he coming here anyway?"

"To give me the results of my test," Stacey replied. "Chandler says—"

Mrs. Linden's brow was still fretted. "Stacey,

do you always call your teachers by their first names?"

Stacey blushed. "Uh, no. He's Mr. Carr."

Both of her parents were now staring at Stacey. Did they sense her feelings for Chandler? They would never approve of Stacey dating an older man, much less her teacher.

Mrs. Linden sighed. "We're just concerned about you, honey. You've seemed different since you started night class."

Stacey knew she had to speak quickly and convincingly. "Yes, I am different, Mom. You were right all along. The age of the dumb model is over. You know, Cindy Crawford was going to be a chemical engineer. She's smart. And I know I need an education, so I'm trying to catch up on my studies."

"And you're sure you're not telling us just what we want to hear?" Mrs. Linden challenged.

"No, Mom. I really want to study hard now. You were right. And I want to know if I have a disability. It's important to me. My school work is coming first from now on."

Mr. Linden shook his head and whistled. "Wow, I can't wait to meet this guy. If he did this in one session—"

The doorbell rang, startling Stacey. Had Chandler arrived already? She didn't see a car in the street when she looked back out the window.

"I'll get it," she said, streaking across the living room to answer the front door.

Chandler Carr was waiting on the front stoop. Stacey almost swooned when she saw him. He was dressed in a black suit, white shirt and a red tie. His hair had been pulled back into a ponytail. But Stacey didn't care about anything except those black eyes that sliced right through her.

"Hi," she said, smiling.

He nodded. "Good evening, Stacey."

"Where's your car?" She asked. "I didn't hear you drive up."

"I don't own a car," he replied. "May I come in?"

Stacey blushed. She realized they were standing there in an awkward moment. She invited him in, closing the door.

Chandler strode into the living room with his easy manner. "Good evening, Mr. and Mrs. Linden. How are you?" His eyes focused on Stacey's mother.

Mrs. Linden immediately smiled, forgetting any doubts she might have had about this handsome man. "How do you do, Mr. Carr?"

"Please, call me Chandler."

Stacey stood behind him, watching as her father came out of his chair. "Hello, Chandler. I hope you don't have too much bad news for us. We're very concerned about Stacey, you know."

Stacey grimaced. "Dad!"

Chandler glanced back at Stacey, dissolving her anxiety with a passing look. "Your father is right," he said to her. "They want to know what your tests show and I don't blame them. Shall we all sit down and discuss it?"

Mr. Linden smiled, taken in by the charisma of this gentleman with dark eyes. "I see why you like him, Stacey. You don't waste any time, Chandler."

Mr. Linden returned to his easy chair. Mrs. Linden sat on the couch. Stacey stood next to Chandler for a moment and then joined her mother on the sofa.

Chandler unfolded a piece of paper that he produced from the inside pocket of his coat. "Now, I'm happy to inform you that Stacey does *not* have a learning disability."

Mr. Linden breathed a sigh of relief. "Thank God."

Mrs. Linden actually applauded. "That's wonderful." She put her arm around Stacey's shoulder.

Stacey had fixed her eyes on her prospective boyfriend. The news about her test results really didn't matter. She just wanted to be around Chandler.

"Now, that doesn't mean that she's out of the woods just yet," Chandler went on. "Years of lazy study habits have taken their toll. I'm afraid her skills are not that of a true high school junior. Someone her age should be further along."

Her age! The words pierced her heart to the quick. He thought of her as a child. *Her age!*

Mr. Linden was frowning now. "What can we do for her to make sure she catches up?"

"I suggest a remedial program," Chandler replied. "She can work with a tutor."

"Can she catch up to senior level by next year?" Mrs. Linden asked in a concerned tone.

Chandler smiled and winked at Stacey. "I think so. And she won't have to come to night class anymore."

"What!" Stacey cried.

Chandler looked at her parents. "She can just as well complete the program in the afternoons. Central has an entire staff of tutors who volunteer from the local junior college. I even know a couple of the students. I could make sure Stacey—"

Stacey stood up, gazing at Chandler with a hurt expression. "I want *you* to tutor me," she said.

Chandler shook his head. "It's not necessary, Stacey."

Stacey turned to her father. "Daddy, I want Chandler to tutor me. Please."

Mr. Linden nodded. "You have done a wonderful job so far, Chandler. Her attitude made an about-face after one class with you. And you are a professional. I don't want some college kid tutoring Stacey."

"Please, Chandler," Mrs. Linden entreated. "I don't want anyone else. I want you."

"If it's a matter of extra money," Mr. Linden started, "then I'm not averse—"

Chandler waved him off. "No, it has nothing to do with money, Mr. Linden. Nothing whatsoever."

Stacey was on the verge of tears. "Then what?"

Chandler sighed. Then he glanced back and forth at Stacey's parents. Suddenly he seemed, sad, forlorn.

Stacey trembled as the tears began to drip from her eyes. Chandler was going to say no. She could see the doleful expression on his adorable face. For a moment, she sensed his deep pain.

He drew another hasty breath. "All right," he said sadly. "I will tutor Stacey myself."

Stacey gasped, "Thank you. Thank you so much." Her feelings of apprehension dissolved into joy.

Mr. Linden smiled broadly. "I knew you'd come through, Chandler. You're a good man."

"I'm going to do well in school," Stacey promised. "I won't disappoint you."

She smiled at Chandler Carr. But he did not return the happy expression. Instead, he lowered his dark eyes and brooded in a way that posed a mystery to Stacey, who was now certain she loved him.

The fog had rolled in again. A dense mist drifted from the Tide Gate River. A round moon flashed between open spaces in the cloud, momentarily lighting the wet grass of the backyard.

Stacey felt herself rising from her bed. She glided toward the dark window casement, which was open. The fog poured into her room, stirred by the chill autumn breeze.

Was her wolf-friend coming tonight? Now that she was in the dream, she was able to remember him. She loved playing with the untamed beast as if he were some kind of excited puppy.

Her eyes peered into the mist. She didn't see him.

In the first dream, she had been the one to hop onto the lawn from her window. But tonight, something told her not to go outside. She was filled with a sense of anticipation, like a visitor was coming tonight, someone very special.

"Chandler," she said, invoking his name like a prayer.

There was a fluttering sound above the house. Mists swirled as a strange creature fell from the sky. Stacey jumped back from the window, closing her eyes.

"I am here," a male voice intoned.

She opened her eyes to see him standing in her room. "Chandler."

She ran to Chandler, embracing him. For a moment, his arms folded around her. She was safe, warm, secure in his embrace.

But then Chandler gently pushed her away from him. "You are so pretty, my lovely Stacey. One of the most beautiful creatures I have ever seen." He touched her chin.

Stacey leaned toward him, her lips pursed. "Kiss me, Chandler. Please—"

He drew back. "Stacey, I can't."

"But don't you think I'm beautiful?"

He sighed, the same plaintive rale that she had heard earlier that evening, before the second night class.

Chandler's eyes were despairing as he gazed into her own. "Stacey, you are so young."

"I don't care," she replied to the dream-shape. "My father is older than my mother."

"It can never be," Chandler replied.

"Why? Why not?" Stacey demanded.

He shook his head gently. "You can never understand my ways. And I have no right to ask you to."

"Don't you love me?" she asked.

"More than anything. But that doesn't always matter. It can never be, Stacey."

She grabbed him, looking into his pale face. "But you love me. And I love you."

He turned away, lifting his hands. "Sacrifices, my love. There are too many sacrifices for us to be together. It can never happen. And you can't expect it to."

"What's wrong?" she asked, her heart filled with trepidation. "Why can't you love me?"

"But I do, that's the hell of it," Chandler said.

"Is it because I'm younger than you?"

He shook his head. "No."

"Chandler—"

He wheeled back, smiling weakly. "My Stacey."

She took his hand, which felt damp and cold. "Chandler, we *can* be together. I don't care what anyone says."

"That's not what bothers me, Stacey. It's the *sacrifice*."

"What sacrifice? For being in love? I don't care, Chandler. I want to be with you."

"No. But we have the night. And we shall use it! Look at me, Stacey."

She did. Stacey felt herself levitating from the floor. Suddenly she was floating out the window into the fog. Chandler held her hand, hovering beside her. In a few minutes, they were flying above the fog, shooting north toward the mountains.

Stacey had never been so free. They soared over the treetops, diving to glide across the moonglow surface of Thunder Lake. Then they went upward, flying to the crest of Mount

Adams. Stacey glanced toward the south. Port City was merely a dim glow on the horizion.

They glided through the air, slowly heading back, descending into the cloud of mist. Stacey found herself standing in her yard. Chandler wrapped his arms around her.

"I must go," he said.

"No!"

"We cannot be together again, my love," Chandler went on. "You are not a creature of the night."

"Yes, yes, I am," she pleaded. "I can be!"

"No. And you will forget this. You will have no recollection of the dream. Now, you will return to your room."

Stacey had become glassy-eyed. "I will return to my room."

In the next instant, she awoke in her bed. For a moment, she thought she heard a fluttering noise outside her room. But when she got up to close the window, the fog was still and silent.

NINE

Stacey glanced up from the paper, gazing into Chandler's black irises. "Wow, I got a seventy-eight. That's better than the last time." The test paper was for a history lesson.

Chandler nodded, wearing the same frown that Stacey had seen for nearly three weeks. It hurt that he was so cold to her. But she had not given up hope. Spending two days a week with him had only whetted her appetite.

"You're doing fine, Stacey," Chandler offered in a dull monotone. "But here, the essay question. You would've gotten an eighty if you had answered it correctly."

Stacey's face wrinkled. "I couldn't think of what to say."

Chandler said, "Okay, in your own words, tell me what the American colonists meant by 'taxation without representation.' Just spell it out."

Stacey took a deep breath, wondering how she could concentrate with Chandler so close to her. Even though the classroom was full of students from the adult program, she still felt like she was alone with him.

"Well," she started, attempting to answer his question, "the colonists didn't want to pay the king without having a say in how and how much they were taxed."

"Exactly," Chandler replied, picking up the paper from her desk. "With that, you get two more points. An eighty is your grade."

Stacey beamed with pride. "That's a B! And I got it on my own. Oh, Chandler—" She reached out to touch his arm, but he drew back, retreating to help another student whose hand was raised.

Stacey almost started crying. How could he ignore her like this? Was she that unattractive to him? It had to be the age thing—and she had to convince him that age didn't matter.

For the rest of the class, Stacey concentrated on her math workbook. She couldn't believe how well she was doing in the remedial program. Had she always been this good in school? Or was it simply Chandler's influence?

She looked up for a moment, focusing on his handsome face. A fantasy played through her head. She was dressed in a fancy ball gown. Chandler asked her to danced. They flew across the floor, swirling, twirling, locked together in a waltz.

"Stacey?"

She glanced up to see him staring at her. "Yes?"

"Class is over," Chandler offered.

She sighed. "Is it?" The room had already emptied.

"Stacey, are you all right?"

Yes, she thought, as long as I'm with you.

"Chandler, I need to talk to you," Stacey said. "Please, it's very important."

He shook his head. "I'm sorry, Stacey. I must go. I must seek nourishment. I haven't eaten all day."

Stacey smiled. "How you talk."

"What?"

"Seek nourishment," she rejoined. "That's a funny way to talk about eating dinner."

"Good night," Chandler told her. "I'll see you again on Tuesday." He made a quick exit from the classroom.

Stacey called after him, "Chandler, wait."

But it was too late. By the time she had followed him into the hallway, he had disappeared. She glanced up and down the dim corridor but saw no sign of him.

"Chandler!"

No reply.

"Chandler, where are you?"

"Chandler, where are you?" came a mocking echo.

Stacey saw someone moving toward her. A male figure slid by the lockers. When he was close enough, Stacey recognized the long hair and handsome face.

"Derek," she said, "what are you doing here?"

Derek put his hands on his hips, striking a cocky pose. "Just checking out night class, babe."

"Did you see my instructor?" she asked quickly.

Derek glared at her. "So that's it, huh? You're hot for this night school geek?"

She leveled her eyes at him. "He's not a geek."

"I saw him," Derek replied. "He's a fancy-faced little prep. I know the type. He doesn't fool me."

"Are you spying on me?" Stacey accused.

"I'm lookin' out for you," Derek replied. "I mean, what does this guy want from you?"

Stacey hung her head. "Apparently nothing."

Derek's face seemed to light up. "So that's it! You're hot for the dweeb-boy, but he's cold for you. Wow, Stace, I thought you were cooler than that."

Stacey turned to walk away from him. "Leave me alone, Derek. I know what I'm doing."

He grabbed her arm. "Don't run away. Hey, if you need someone to ice you down, I'm your man."

Stacey shrugged out of his grip. "Forget it, Derek. We're history. You never meant anything to me."

He grabbed her shoulders this time. "Look at me."

Stacey's eyes lifted to meet his steely gaze. "What?"

"You've really got it bad for this guy," Derek said. "Little Miss Ice Princess has a melting heart."

"Let go of me!" Stacey struggled to free herself from his grasp. She finally wriggled out of the hold he had on her. When her arms were free, she slapped him squarely across the face.

Derek flinched, touching his stinging cheek. "You hit me!"

Stacey was going to tell him off, but Derek swung the flat of his hand, slapping her in the mouth. Stacey stumbled backward, holding her hands over her face. A slight trickle of warm blood flowed onto her fingertips.

"You've lost it!" Stacey said, backing away, bumping into the lockers. "You're ballistic, Derek."

He took a step in her direction, a pained look on his face. "Stacey, I—you hit me first!"

She thrust out her hand. "Stay away! I mean it."

"What's with you!" Derek cried. "You'll give it to this little geek—"

"I'm not doing anything with Chandler," Stacey replied. "He doesn't want me. And I don't want *you*."

"This guy is trouble," Derek warned. "I mean it, Stacey. Forget about him."

"You're just jealous, Derek!"

He came at her again. "Stacey—"

She broke into a run, sprinting as fast as she could toward the exit. Derek chased her. He managed to catch Stacey before she reached the end of the hallway.

"Listen to me," Derek went on as he wrestled with her, "he's too old for you. I'm the one you should be with, Stacey."

"I'm going to scream, Derek. Let go of me or I'll—"

"Hey, what's going on here!"

The male voice echoed through the corridor.

Stacey glanced at the figure in the shadows. "Chandler?"

But it was only a janitor, a night worker at Central. He squinted at Derek, who immediately let go of Stacey. Derek stepped back a few paces, looking guilty and sheepish.

The janitor, a kind-faced man with graying hair, came up closer to them. "Son, that's no way to treat a lady."

"I'm not your son," Derek replied. "And she's no lady!"

Before the older gentleman could say another word, Derek bolted from the hallway, running outside.

Stacey drew in a fearful breath. "Thank you."

"Got to be careful these days," he told her. "Would you like me to walk you to your car?"

She shook her head. "No, thanks. My mother is waiting for me. I'll be all right."

Stacey fled into the cold night. It was early November, almost time for winter. A stiff wind blew over Port City, rattling windows and creaking tree boughs.

As Stacey hurried across the campus, she saw the lights of her mother's car. For a moment, she thought she heard something above her head, a fluttering sound like the beating of wings. But the weird noise quickly disappeared.

Derek stopped in a dark corner of Rockbury Lane, catching his breath. He hadn't figured on the old janitor showing up. What a lousy break. He had hoped to talk some sense into Stacey about the crush she had on her teacher. It was doomed.

When Derek was breathing easier, he began to walk toward the park. He regretted having slapped Stacey. It had been a reflex after she had hit him. But there was no excuse for it. It didn't take much courage to slap a girl.

Derek crossed Middle Road, entering Fair Common Park. The wind chilled the back of his neck. He turned up the collar on his leather jacket. It was a long walk to Pitney Docks, but he had some steam to work off.

He really loved Stacey. But she was a spoiled

little rich girl from Prescott Estates, and it was probably stupid to try and keep her. After all, her father was probably going to be mayor of Port City someday. He certainly wouldn't want his little princess hanging out with a long-hair who played in a rock-and-roll band.

As Derek reached the midpoint of the park, he heard something overhead. Wings seemed to appear from the sky. Then something sharp brushed his face, scratching him.

"Ow, what the—" Blood trickled down his cheek. "Sea gulls!"

Gulls sometimes got too aggressive with humans, though Derek had never known it to happen at night. He kept walking, casting an eye to the dark heavens. It was a crazy evening. He just wanted to get home and lock the door.

He had gone a few more steps when he heard a low growling in front of him.

Derek stopped dead in his tracks. Was that the shady silhouette of a dog? Or a wolf?

He backpedaled a couple of feet. "Whoa, good doggy—I—"

The wolf charged at him.

Derek turned to run but he wasn't fast enough. The wolf flew into the air, hitting Derek in the back with its paws. Derek tumbled to the ground, expecting the animal to bite him.

But instead, the wolf just seemed to disappear.

"What the—"

A man was standing over him now.

Derek stared into the obscure face. "Hey, did you see that dog? Man, it was creepy!"

Derek tried to get up, but a strong hand knocked him down.

"What's the big idea!"

"You will sleep," a spooky voice commanded.

"No, I—"

But Derek's eyelids had suddenly grown leaden.

As he closed his eyes, the man bent to touch the blood that trickled from the scratch on his cheek.

In her dream, Stacey waited by the window. No one had come for a while, but tonight she was filled by a sense of expectation. There was no mist in the backyard. It was too cold for the fog now.

Stacey gazed up at a moonless sky. Why did she expect her loved one to come from the heavens? If only he would arrive to wrap his arms around her.

Suddenly, she heard fluttering in the sky. She lowered her eyes to see him standing there. He was clad in a loose-fitting white shirt and a pair of black trousers.

"You came!" she said.

Chandler nodded. "I had to see you."

As in her other dream, Stacey found herself floating through the air. When she touched the ground, she embraced him. Chandler held her close to his chest.

"I love you," she told him. "Don't you love me?"

He said, "More than the moon and the stars."

She peered into the nightshade of his eyes. "Kiss me!"

He put a finger to her lips. "Not yet. I must tell you, I did not like the way that boy man-handled you."

Stacey laughed. "Derek? Forget him. Kiss me."

"The temptation is too great," he replied. Chandler lowered his lips to her mouth. When their lips met, Stacey felt a jolt. Chandler seemed to draw out her soul. They were inter-twined, one being, locked forever in a passion-ate embrace.

Chandler drew back suddenly. "No more."

"But I *want* you to kiss me," Stacey replied. "Please, I've never been kissed like that before."

"Nor will you be again," Chandler replied.

"What?"

He lowered his head, sad and distant. "It still cannot be, Stacey. The sacrifice—"

"What sacrifice?" she asked. "Chandler, there's nothing that you can say or do to make me stop loving you."

He shook his head slowly. "You would not enjoy my fate, Stacey. And I cannot condemn you to it."

"What fate?" she went on in a desperate voice. "Chandler, love is the only thing that—"

"No!"

"Please, Chandler—"

She started toward him. Chandler held out his hand. Stacey immediately felt his power. She stopped dead, unable to take another step.

"You will forget this, like the others," Chandler told her.

Her eyes were glazed over. "I will forget."

He touched her soft face for a moment. "Forgive me, Stacey. Forgive me for what I have had to do."

She heard the words in her head.

Then she sat up in bed, shivering.

Cold air filled her room.

She had to rise to close the window.

Her eyes peered into the darkness of her backyard. Had she been dreaming again? Why couldn't she remember?

Stacey shut the window, climbed back into bed, listening to the unsettled whining of the wind.

TEN

When Stacey walked into the kitchen the next day, her father looked up from his morning paper and smiled. "Hi, Princess, I hear you got an eighty on a quiz."

Stacey plopped down at the breakfast table, nodding absently. She gave a wide yawn and shook her head. Though she could not remember her dreams of Chandler, the restless nights were taking their toll.

Her mother moved away from the kitchen sink, putting her hand on Stacey's forehead. "Are you running a temperature?"

Stacey grimaced, pulling back. "Mom! I'm okay."

Mr. Linden studied his daughter closely. "Honey, you do look a little pale. Maybe you should stay home from school today."

"No," Stacey insisted.

She couldn't miss school. Chandler wouldn't like it. She had to keep working hard at her studies. Maybe he might love her when she was smarter, as smart as he.

Mrs. Linden smiled. "Well, Stacey, I have to tell you how pleased I am with your progress. Mr. Carr seems to be doing a great job. But are you sure this night class thing isn't a bit too much for you?"

"Mom!" Stacey made a face. "I'm all right."

Mrs. Linden eased toward the sink. "Okay, okay. Don't snap my head off. You haven't talked to me like that since you were fourteen, Stacey."

"I'm sorry," Stacey replied. "I'm just cranky this morning. Okay? Is that all right with everyone?"

Mr. Linden shrugged. "Fine with me." He dug into his paper again, turning to the Port City Metro section.

Stacey nibbled at toast and eggs. She finished her orange juice but didn't touch the bacon. Why did she feel so tired? Had she been dreaming of Chandler? Her head whirred with dark images that were indecipherable.

Mrs. Linden sat down next to Stacey. "Would you like to invite Mr. Carr to the house again?" she asked.

Stacey sat up straight, trying not to sound to eager. "Uh, sure, why not?"

Maybe she could make some progress with him on her own turf. He had to know that she was mature beyond her seventeen years. If they spent a quiet evening together, he might come around. . . .

"Goodness," Mr. Linden said suddenly, stumbling over a story in the newspaper. "I don't believe it."

Mrs. Linden glanced toward the open page. "What is it?"

Mr. Linden cast his eyes in the direction of his daughter. "Stacey, didn't you know a boy named Derek Barton?"

"Yes," Stacey replied.

"He's dead," Mr. Linden told her. "He hanged himself in Fair Common Park last night."

Stacey's brow wrinkled. "Derek?"

"Yes. He left a suicide note."

Stacey sighed, oddly detached. "That's too bad."

"Didn't you date him?" Mrs. Linden asked.

Stacey shrugged. "Yes, a little. But I haven't seen him for a while."

"Was he the type to do something like this?" Mr. Linden asked. "To kill himself?"

Stacey took a deep breath and then exhaled like she was bored. "I don't know."

Her parents looked at each other. Their daughter seemed strangely unconcerned about the death of a classmate. And a suicide at that.

Stacey looked down at her scrambled eggs. She could barely remember what Derek had looked like, as if someone had managed to erase her memory. She didn't care about Derek. But she thought she had come up with a plan to get closer to Chandler.

At the end of fourth period, Stacey went to Mr. Kinsley's office. It was her lunch time, so she was able to wait until he could see her. Mr. Kinsley smiled from behind his desk. He actually seemed glad that Stacey had come to visit him.

"I hear you're doing very well," Kinsley went on. "You didn't have a learning disability at all, as it turns out."

"No, I didn't, Mr. Kinsley—"

But the smile left his thin face, replaced by a grim expression. "When I see how much you've improved, Stacey—well, it just makes me feel worse about Derek Barton. Didn't you use to date him, Stacey?"

She sighed, lowering her eyes for a moment. "A little. I do feel sorry for him."

"I'm not closing the school," the vice-principal said. "Not for something like this. It's better that we just keep going. I don't want to encourage any students to think of—well, you know."

Stacey glanced up again, nodding, focusing her charms on the red-haired man. "Mr. Kinsley, I wanted to thank you for helping me. It was just what I needed. You saved me."

He smiled sheepishly, affecting modesty. "Well, that's quite all right, Stacey—"

"Night school has been wonderful," Stacey

went on. "I've really turned it around. It's just—"

She gave a little frown, pouting.

Mr. Kinsley snapped on the baited hook. "What's wrong, Stacey? Is it something I can help with?"

Opening her notebook, Stacey took out a folder full of blank paper. "It's this paper I've been working on. A special report. And I forgot to give it to Mr. Carr. He's supposed to grade it this weekend. Only it's Friday, so there's no class tonight. And I just have to get it to him. It's a big part of my remedial studies."

Mr. Kinsley grimaced. "I'm sorry, Stacey. You're right, there's no night classes on Friday. Thank God it's Friday, though. This thing with the Barton kid has shaken everyone. There's going to be a special memorial service for him on Sunday, by the way."

"I plan to go," Stacey offered. "Uh, I was wondering, Mr. Kinsley, if there was any way I could get this paper to Mr. Carr. If I knew his home address—"

Kinsley snapped his fingers. "Sure, Stacey. No problem."

She shrugged. "I mean, I don't really have to even go there. If I dropped it in the mail today, he'd get it tomorrow."

Kinsley was already checking his Rolodex file on the top of his desk. "No problem, Stacey. I understand. Here, one-thirteen North Division

Road. That's out near you, Stacey. Isn't North Division Road on the other end of Prescott Estates?"

"Yes, it is," Stacey said, writing down the address. "Thank you, Mr. Kinsley."

She got up, heading for the door.

"Stacey?"

"Yes?" she replied, turning back to face him.

He exhaled, grimacing sadly. "This Barton kid. Are you sure you didn't know something about him? Something that might have led him to—you know?"

She shook her head. "No, sir. He must've been very troubled to do something like that. But I only went out with him once or twice. He just wasn't my type."

"I understand. I want you to know how happy I am for you, Stacey. Don't let this horrible incident interfere with your own progress."

Stacey feigned deep sympathy, frowning and looking at the floor. "I won't, Mr. Kinsley. I promise."

She left quickly, darting into the hall.

Stacey held up the address and read it aloud. She had it. Now she knew where to find Chandler Carr.

Stacey's Geo Tracker rolled slowly along North Division Road. It was almost four o'clock. The winter sun hung low over the horizon, casting a reddish pallor onto Port City.

Stacey's heart raced as she watched the house numbers. She put on the brakes in front of one-thirteen. Chandler lived in a Victorian-style house that had not been kept up very well.

A car stopped behind Stacey's Tracker, honking its horn. Stacey had to move. She pulled over to the curb, letting the other car pass. Stacey glanced toward the house, her head spinning.

How was she going to approach him? Just knock on the door and say, "Here I am." Would he turn her away?

Stacey began to feel like a fool. After all, she didn't want to stalk him! She put the Tracker in gear and roared off away from one-thirteen North Division Road.

But she didn't go home. Stacey couldn't bring herself to drive back to her own house. She just kept passing back and forth in front of Chandler's house. With each trip, the shadows grew deeper and deeper around the old place. Stacey was waiting for the lights to go on.

Why couldn't she leave him alone? Because he was the most fascinating man she had ever met. She had to try. But how? Just walk up to his door and knock?

Yes! A walk. She could pretend to be taking a walk, pass his house as he came out, make it seem like a chance meeting. Then she could at least talk to him.

She steered the Tracker to the curb about a

half mile away from Chandler's place. She could tell him that she had walked from her house. Even though North Division Road was an older section of Prescott Estates, it was technically part of her neighborhood. Didn't she have a right to walk where she pleased?

Leaving the Tracker, she started along the sidewalk on weak, wobbly legs. She could barely find her strength. The thought of actually talking to him made her queasy. Yet, she had to do it. She had to know if there was a chance.

The streetlights were beginning to glow as she approached his house. There were no signs of life inside the dark dwelling. Stacey didn't want to wait on the sidewalk, so kept moving.

As she passed Chandler's house, she thought she heard someone behind her, scuffling on the sidewalk. But when she turned to look for Chandler, she saw only a fleeting shadow that may or may not have been an intruder. Was that someone ducking behind a hedge?

Stacey kept walking, crossing the street to slip between the spreading branches of two spruce trees. When she turned around, she could see Chandler's house. It was the perfect place to watch for him. Then she would stroll out onto the sidewalk and chalk up their meeting to happenstance.

Her heart soared when a light flashed on in Chandler's front windows. For a moment she smiled, at least until she noticed the shadow creeping at the edge of the house. Was there an intruder trying to peek through the window?

Stacey squinted, watching as the shadows disappeared. It had to be a trick of the streetlight. Who would want to bother Chandler? Except herself, that is.

For a long time, she waited for the front door to open. Finally, Chandler Carr made his exit from the house. He was clad in a long, dark woolen coat that covered everything but his hands, his feet and his head. Chandler's gorgeous face appeared pale and worn in the streetlights. Another trick of the night, Stacey thought.

She stepped out from her hiding place in the trees, hoping to rendezvous with the man she loved.

ELEVEN

"Chandler!" Stacey called as she crossed the street. "How are you? I was just—"

Chandler flinched when he heard her voice. His dark eyes lifted to peer at her through the evening shadows. A grim expression covered his pale face. Stacey stopped for a second, squinting at him. He didn't look the same somehow. He seemed older, more worn around the eyes.

"Chandler?" she asked hesitantly.

The shine was gone from his eyes. There was no luster in his thick hair, which now appeared to be streaked with strands of gray. What had happened to him? Why was he dressed so strangely?

Chandler turned his face away from her, starting along the sidewalk, fleeing with his back to her.

"Chandler?" She stepped onto the sidewalk. "Chandler, what—"

"Leave me alone, Stacey," he called in a cracking voice. "Please, leave me alone!"

"Chandler, I just wanted to talk!"

She went after him, but he broke into a run. "Chandler!"

She tried to catch him. Chandler was very quick on his feet. Stacey saw him duck into an alley between two houses. She followed him into the alley, squinting in the shadows.

"Chandler?"

Stacey eased back into the darkness, wondering why he had run from her. "Chandler, I was just taking a walk when I saw you. I'm not—I mean, you *can* talk to me, can't you?"

No reply from the blackness.

When Stacey had gone a little farther, she saw that the alley way was a dead end. "Chandler?"

Nothing from the shadows.

"Chandler, where did you go?"

He couldn't have disappeared into thin air. Did he jump over the fence at the end of the alley?

"Chandler, are you—"

Something fluttered above Stacey's head. She heard a squeaking and then the flapping of leathery wings. It was a sound she half-remembered from her dreams.

"Chandler—"

But he was no longer there. He had probably leapt over the fence to get away from her.

Stacey's face went slack in a desperate frown. Tears began to form in her eyes.

He hated her! That had to be the answer. He hated her so much that he wanted to be rid of her.

With pearls of sorrow streaking down her cheeks, Stacey turned to leave the alleyway. She didn't have a chance with Chandler now. If he despised her that much—hadn't he suggested that she complete her remedial program during the day, so he wouldn't have to be around her—why did he let her stay in his class?

And the dreams!

Stacey stopped for a second in the alley, shivering in the frigid night air. Suddenly she remembered the dreams. Chandler had come to her in the mist.

Were they dreams? Or wishful thinking on her part?

Or were they real?

Chandler certainly had some strange effect on her. After all, why else would she be standing in a dark alley on a cold November night? Chasing a man she hardly knew . . .

For the first time in a long while, Stacey was feeling like her old self. Her mind was working in that selfish way she had known before meeting Chandler. She had been going about this all wrong. She had never gotten anything by pussyfooting around, by acting like a weepy wallflower.

Stacey had always achieved her goals with trickery or direct confrontation. Why should now be any different? If she wanted Chandler, she'd have to go after him in an aggressive way.

But why had he run? And why had he looked so horribly drawn and exhausted? He had always seemed so young before.

Stacey started forward again. It all seemed so significant and unreal. Yet, she had to have the answers to her questions. How else would she be able to resolve her unrequited love for Chandler Carr? She had to confront him with her feelings sooner or later.

Stacey looked up to see the dim glow of the streetlights framing the entrance to the alleyway. She had almost reached the street when the male figure stepped into the light. Stacey smiled, thinking that Chandler had returned.

"You came back!" she cried. "Chandler—"

"No," the voice told her. "It's not Chandler."

A frost crept into Stacey's bones. She could not identify the intruder's face with the light shining behind him. Was this the same man who had been following her earlier? The dark shadow she had seen at the edge of Chandler's house, peering in the window?

"Are you Stacey Linden?" the intruder asked in a grave tone.

Stacey did not reply. She inched back a few

steps until she realized that she was heading for a dead end. The only way out of the alley was to go *through* the encroaching shadowman.

He started toward her. "Are you Stacey Linden?" he repeated.

Stacey felt a burning sensation in her throat. She could not have spoken if she had wanted to. A surge of adrenaline coursed through her body, readying her.

Nowhere to run.

Why was he following her?

Just get away, she told herself.

He was almost on her. "I need to see Stacey Linden!"

Stacey charged the intruder, slamming her fists into his chest. The man had been relaxed, not expecting her to fight back. Stacey's charge sent him toppling. He tumbled to the gravel-strewn surface of the alley.

"No!" the intruder cried, grabbing his leg. "Don't run! I have to talk to you!"

Stacey leapt over him, flying toward the street. She turned onto the sidewalk, running in the direction of the Tracker. It wasn't far. But then she heard the male voice behind her.

"Stop! I just want to—ow, my ankle. Please!"

Stacey saw the Tracker ahead. She jumped inside and roared away from her attacker's cries. If the man hadn't hurt his ankle, there was every chance he would've caught her.

As she guided the Tracker through Prescott

Estates, Stacey wondered why the intruder had been hanging around Chandler's place. Was it possible Chandler was in some kind of trouble?

What if Chandler had some sort of horrible skeleton in his closet? Was he really capable of doing something heinous and wrong? Stacey couldn't believe that Chandler would harm a soul. Certainly, he had been nothing less than a gentleman with her.

Stacey's spirits sank suddenly. Chandler had shunned her. He had rejected her in a way that no other guy had ever done. No! She could not give in to a broken heart.

"There has to be a way," she said aloud.

What difference did it make if Chandler was in trouble? Her father was a big man in Port City. Surely her father could help Chandler. Somebody had to help him if he really needed it.

As she approached her own house, she considered asking her father to help right away. But when she finally entered the living room to see him reading a book in his easy chair, Stacey just said hello. She didn't want to play this hand too early.

"Aren't you coming home a little late?" Mr. Linden asked.

Stacey shrugged. "Sorry, I had to get some books from my locker."

Mr. Linden nodded. "Oh. How's it going?"

"Fine," Stacey replied. "I have to study."

"Okay, Princess."

Stacey hurried to the privacy of her own bedroom. She fell on the bed, crying for a while. When she finally dried her eyes, Stacey rose and went to the window. Gazing into the dark, cold night, she once again arrived at the same conclusion.

If she was going to resolve this aching in her soul, she had to face Chandler.

And she had to face him tonight.

A brisk wind whipped down the sidewalk, stinging Stacey's face as she neared Chandler's house. Her heart was pumping. She expected the intruder to be on her again, leaping from the dense shadows that surrounded the house.

She didn't care. She'd face any danger to be with Chandler. She wanted him more than any boy she had ever known. Chandler was a man. She'd convince him that they were right for each other.

Stacey hadn't expected the door to be open, and it wasn't. She had to use a rock to break a pane of glass in the front door so she could reach in to unlock the deadbolt. As she was pulling her hand from the hole in the door, she cut her index finger on a shard of glass.

"Damn!"

She put her finger in her mouth as she eased into the shrouded rooms. The place had an exotic, musty scent. Stacey started forward in the shadows. She knew that Chandler wasn't home yet. She'd find a place to sit and wait for him.

Stacey found a light switch on the wall. She was standing in a room full of books, shelves on every wall. Chandler had to be brilliant to have read so many books.

Gazing at his private den, Stacey was suddenly filled with a sense of curiosity. She wanted to know *everything* about Chandler. And what better way to find out than to take a tour of his house?

Stacey passed from the library to another small room that was empty. She entered a corridor that took her a few steps into a spotless kitchen. She had to smile. A typical male—he probably had beer and hot dogs in the refrigerator. Stacey just had to peek.

When she opened the refrigerator door, however, her face tensed into an expression of confusion and disbelief. "What the—"

Small plastic pint-sized bags rested on the wire shelves of refrigerator. Stacey picked up one of the bags, reading the white printing: FOR BLOOD STORAGE ONLY. There had to be more than three dozen bags, all empty except for a crimson residue inside.

"Blood storage?" she asked herself aloud.

Why did Chandler need blood? Was he a

hemophiliac? Stunned she closed the door and turned away from her eerie discovery.

She didn't think she could wait for Chandler in the kitchen now. Stacey staggered a bit, her legs weak. She opened another door at the end of the short hallway. Was this Chandler's bedroom? Maybe she shouldn't be here.

She had to look, however, even if she didn't wait there. Her finger flipped a switch on the wall. Immediately, Stacey wished that she had stayed in the kitchen. A lone object rested on the floor in the center of the room. Stacey had never been to a funeral, but she knew a coffin when she saw one.

"My God!"

The lid of the coffin was open. Stacey bent down to touch the cool soil that lay in the bottom of the casket. What on earth was Chandler doing? He had to be sick to be sleeping in a dirt-filled coffin. Or was this some insane game?

"Good evening, Stacey."

She almost jumped into the coffin. When she spun around, she saw Chandler standing in front of her. His skin was now firm and white. The sheen had returned to his hair. And he had returned to his home.

"Now you know," he said to Stacey.

She could not speak. Until she looked into his eyes. The irises whirled and danced with the obscure, ink-black flow. Chandler had beauty beyond the world.

Suddenly, Stacey wasn't afraid anymore. "Hello, my love," she said in a breathy voice.

Chandler replied, "Welcome home."

TWELVE

Once again, Stacey was enraptured by the beauty in Chandler's black eyes. She could not look away. The swirling irises pierced the depths of her soul, drawing her in, making her forget the bizarre discoveries in his house. There had to be an explanation for the empty blood packets and the dirt-filled coffin. And he would explain it all to her now, he would convince her that he was not a monster, that she was right to love him.

Stacey put her hand on his soft face. "My love."

He no longer looked drawn and sallow. She ran her hand along his neck, touching his shiny hair. He was so handsome. And she would have him now and forever.

He took her hand, kissing the fingertips. "You are lovely, my Stacey. A creature of such beauty."

She smiled. *"Your* Stacey?"

He sighed. "I wish it were so. But the sacrifice—"

Her eyes widened. "Sacrifice," she said. "I remember the dreams now. They were dreams, weren't they?"

Chandler touched her cheek with the back of his hand. "No, my love. They weren't dreams. I really came to you. I had to kiss you. I had to be with you. I'm in love with you, Stacey. I love you more than my horrible, wretched existence."

Stacey gently shook her head. "No. It can't be that bad. Whatever it is—Chandler you must tell me. If we're going to be together, I have to know."

She couldn't believe what she was saying. There were so many unanswered questions. But she was in a trance, captured again by his power.

Chandler let go of her hand and turned away. "Stacey, you can never understand. Please, don't press me. If you do . . . I will be unable to resist you. My love for you—well, it has been some time since I have experienced emotions like this."

She grabbed his shoulders, spinning him toward her, embracing him, burying her face in his chest. "Oh, Chandler. I don't want you to resist me. I've waited so long to hear you say you love me. Now that I'm sure, I can't let you go."

Tenderly, he pushed her away. "Stacey, I don't know where to start. How can I tell you—"

"You said the dreams were real," Stacey said. "Why couldn't I remember them until now?"

He smiled, tilting his head. "Stacey, I have certain—abilities. I willed that you wouldn't remember, so you didn't."

"Abilities. Yes, I can see that. Chandler, why did you run from me tonight?"

"I sought nourishment," he replied.

"Is that why you looked different?"

He nodded. "Stacey, you looked in the refrigerator. What did you find? "

"Blood packets," she said. "Chandler—"

"And the coffin," he went on. "Did you see it? The sacred earth from my grave?"

She chortled nervously. "Chandler, don't play a joke on me. Please, don't—"

"This is no joke, Stacey. If you want to know everything about me, I must be honest."

Stacey felt a fluttering in the pit of her stomach. "Chandler, I'm afraid. Please—"

But when he peered at her again, the fears dissolved. He did have some strange hold on her. And Stacey was certain that she didn't want him to free her.

"Stacey," he went on, "your friend Derek. And that man who attacked you the first night you came to my class."

"They're dead," Stacey replied.

"Yes, my love. They are dead. And tomorrow, another body will be found in Port City. It will seem like a mysterious murder, unexplainable."

"Chandler—"

The fear swelled and then vanished. She could not remain scared with him gazing at her. How could she be afraid with those black eyes penetrating her very being?

"I don't expect you to understand, Stacey. It is too much to ask of you. I could never expect you to—"

"Chandler, just tell me—"

But she already knew. She simply had to hear it from him. The words would not sting her. She was too much in love, caught in his hypnotic trance.

"Stacey, I'm a creature of the night," Chandler replied softly, staring into her eyes. "I must seek the blood of others to live."

"You killed Derek," she said.

"He hurt you," Chandler replied. "I could not let him get away with that."

Stacey glanced aside for a moment. Chandler had just confessed to killing Derek. Why didn't she feel some remorse, some sense of outrage? His dark, piercing eyes called her back, erasing all logic, all morality. He had a grip on her and Stacey was powerless to resist him.

"Don't hate me, Stacey," he told her in a soothing tone. "I have to feed. If I don't, well— you don't want to know what will happen to me if I don't."

A chill swept over Stacey. She put a hand to her throat, shivering. "Chandler—I—I don't know what to say. It's confusing."

"Of course it is, my dear," he replied, lifting her chin to mesmerize her. "I am a creature like no other you have ever known. And I cannot expect you to make the sacrifice—"

She should have been repulsed. She should have run away from the house, never to see him again. But he had her soul in chains. His powers were too great. And those black eyes!

"What sacrifice are you talking about?" she asked hesitantly.

"You can be with me," Chandler replied. "But to be with me, you must also be *like* me."

"Be like you?"

A creature of the night. Wasn't that what he said? She would have to be like him. Was the sacrifice worth it?

Chandler grimaced. "Oh, my Stacey. Can't you see how I have agonized over loving you?"

She nodded slowly. "Yes, I can feel your pain."

His eyes never left hers as he put forth his argument. "Can you imagine what it is like to never feel the sun on your face? I cannot walk with your kind."

"My kind?" she repeated.

"Humans, Stacey. You can see now that I am not of your world. I must live in darkness. I must seek my nourishment from the blood of others. I must—"

"A vampire," Stacey said softly. "You're a vampire."

A sudden expression of rage came over his face. Stacey felt his temper. He shook her violently.

"Never use that word to describe me!" Chandler cried. "Do you hear me! Never!"

Tears welled in her deep blue eyes. "I'm sorry. I never meant to hurt you. I—"

He embraced her, pulling Stacey close to him. "My love, I didn't mean to talk to you like that. I—there is so much mortals cannot understand."

Pressed against his chest, Stacey suddenly felt revulsion and loathing for him. But when he gazed into her eyes again, the ill feelings vanished. She could only love him with their eyes locked.

Yet, there were so many things she had to know. "Chandler, do you—I mean, do you actually, you know, bite them on the neck and suck out the blood?"

His face grew pale and distant. For a moment, she thought he was going to get angry again. But he only smiled at her, a weird, otherworldly leer. Stacey took the expression to be an indication of his love and affection.

"You grow curious," Chandler said. "Could it be that I was wrong about you?"

"You know I love you," Stacey replied, her emotions captive to his spell. "Tell me how it works. How you're a vam— I mean, how you do it."

He stroked her hair, gazing into her expectant face. "Eternal life," he told her. "To live forever. To never die."

"But you said it was horrible," she offered.

"Not with you by my side," he replied. "To love you forever. To have you as my bride. The nights would not seem so long."

"Wow. To never die." She glanced away for a second, but he pulled her back. "I love you, Chandler."

"And I love you," he replied. "Are you prepared, Stacey? Are you ready to live with me forever? To be the queen of the night."

"Chandler—"

She hesitated. Something inside her told Stacey to run. But the black eyes had imprisoned her. And Chandler refused to let her go.

"You must come with me willingly, Stacey. I could not bear to live with myself if you did not come willingly. Please, say you'll be my bride."

Her face felt feverish. How could she say no to

him? She loved him. She wanted to be with him
forever.

"Will I have to—to drink blood too?" she
asked.

He laughed. "You have nothing to worry
about, Stacey. If you don't love me—"

"But I do!"

"If you don't want to be my bride—"

She wrapped her arms around him. "Yes,
Chandler, I want to marry you. I want to stay
with you forever."

"I must take from you," Chandler told her.
"Our blood must mingle. I must drink from the
fountain of your soul."

Stacey shivered as he swept the hair away
from her neck. "Chandler—" Was this right?
Did she really want him to do this?

"Silent, my love. It will not hurt you."

"Chandler, I don't know—"

She started to draw back. He pulled her
closer, lowering his mouth toward her neck.
Stacey's heart pounded in her chest. It was all
happening so fast.

"You and I will be one forever!"

Stacey glanced over his shoulder. She could
not see his reflection in the mirrored glass
across the room. He really *was* a vampire. And
he was about to make her one too!

"Chandler, please don't—I—"

She couldn't pull back. He was too strong. His

lips brushed the soft skin of her neck. Were those pointed teeth pressing against her?

"Chandler—" She struggled with him. "Please—"

"You will be a goddess of the night, my love!"

"That's what you think, Chandler!"

The pointed fangs pulled away before they pierced her skin. Chandler let go of Stacey, turning to face the voice that had come from behind them. Stacey fell back with her hand to her throat.

"You!" Chandler cried. "You come to plague me again!"

"More than you know," the male voice boomed. "More than you know, brother!"

Stacey recognized the voice. It was the same person who had accosted her earlier that evening.

Chandler made a hissing sound. "You will die!" he cried.

"I don't think so," the young man replied.

Chandler took a step toward him. But the young man raised a golden cross that was ringed with bulbs of garlic. Chandler cried out and covered his face.

"No!" Stacey shrieked. "Don't hurt him!"

He kept the crucifix in front of him as he moved toward Stacey. Chandler cowered against the wall, shielding his face, shrinking away in revulsion from the religious icon. The young man grabbed Stacey's hand.

She tried to shake his grip. "No, I want to stay with Chandler. I love him."

"You stay with Chandler and you'll be one of the walking dead," he snapped. "Let's go!"

"I'll kill you!" Chandler threatened. "I swear it."

The young man brandished the golden cross as he dragged Stacey past a trembling Chandler. "Not tonight, brother."

Chandler hissed and bared his teeth. Stacey caught a glimpse of his wolfish, hideous face—a mask of hatred now. He wasn't the handsome night class teacher anymore. He was an ugly monster who had killed her friend. And he wouldn't killed her, too . . . or worse.

"Hurry!" the young man cried.

Stacey followed him through the dark house. They burst out into the yard, running for their lives. When they hit the street, they turned in the direction of her Tracker.

"We'll take your car," he told her.

"How did you know where—"

"I've been following you," he said.

He grabbed her hand again. "We need to get away from here as fast as we can."

They flew toward the Tracker, climbing in. Stacey put the car in gear and roared down North Division Road. Her head was spinning, confused, jumbled by the insane things that had happened to her this night.

"Who are you?" she asked the young man next to her.

"William," he replied. "My friends call me Will."

"But who—"

"I'm William Carr," he replied with a grimace. "Chandler's younger brother."

THIRTEEN

Stacey glanced sideways at the young man who sat in the passenger seat. "Chandler's brother? But he said he was going to kill you. That he was going to—"

"I know, I know. I've heard it all before. Watch the road."

Stacey turned her eyes forward. Her head throbbed and her lips were trembling. What has happened to her? Why had she almost been willing to let Chandler turn her into the living dead?

"You're not his brother!" Stacey accused. "You just want to hurt him!"

"What do you think he was going to do back there?" Will Carr challenged. "He wasn't going to ask you to the prom, Stacey. He was going to kill you."

"I—I love him," Stacey replied. "And he says he loves mc. Like no other person he's ever known."

Will chortled derisively. "You think so, huh? Do you know how many girls like you have bought that line?"

Stacey blushed. She caught a glimpse of Will's face in the rearview mirror. He did resemble Chandler. Will had lighter hair and flashing green eyes. He was also stockier than Chandler, but it was all muscle. Stacey might have thought he was attractive under different circumstances.

"He loves me!" she insisted. "Chandler and I are—"

Will lifted his finger, interrupting her. "Let me see if I know the drill. Okay, you're in his night class, right? You think he's the cutest thing since boxer shorts. Only, he's real shy at first. Doesn't want to talk to you."

Stacey's jaw went slack, her mouth dropping open. How did Will know all these things? It was just like he described it.

"So the big 'C' has you, right? He can do this whammy thing with his eyes. You know, kind of like Obiewan Kenobe in *Star Wars*. Only he's really Darth Vader. The Prince of Freakin' Darkness."

"No," Stacey replied, though she was losing some of her steam.

"He's got you," Will went on. "You're hooked. And he would've reeled you in soon enough. Only you surprised him. You came looking and he wasn't ready for you."

"I surprised him?" Stacey asked.

"Yeah, he picked a real go-getter this time," Will replied. "And a looker too. I gotta say, you're gorgeous, Stacey. Did he give you the one about being the queen of his realm?"

Stacey's mouth tightened. "Stop it!"

"What about that guy they fished from the river?" Will challenged. "And your friend Derek?"

Stacey started to cry all of a sudden. Derek was gone. How could she have been so callous to not care about his death?

"It was Chandler," Will said, as if he had read her mind. "He had you hypnotized, Stacey. And you had dreams, didn't you?"

"How did you know about the dreams?"

Will grimaced and moaned. "You think I'm a fool? I know how he operates. He's my brother!"

"You couldn't know about my dreams."

"They weren't dreams, Stacey."

She shuddered, remembering Chandler's confession. "No, they weren't."

"He was there," Will insisted. "First he came as a wolf, didn't he?"

"How did you—"

"Vampires can change into wolves or bats," he replied. "I know, I did my research."

"This can't be happening, Will. It can't."

He gestured to the curb. "Pull over."

"What?"

"Just pull over."

Stacey guided the Tracker next to the curb. "What's wrong?"

Will turned to face her. "I'm sorry I have to do this, Stacey. It's not my style."

"What're you—"

Will slapped her. It wasn't hard, but the tips of his fingers stung her cheeks. As Stacey sobbed, Will wrapped his arms around her, drawing her close.

"Okay," he whispered, "you're gonna come to your senses. He's a killer, honey."

"I know," Stacey muttered. "I know."

"He's already killed two people in Port City, and he's probably killed another one tonight."

"For their blood," Stacey moaned. "He's a vampire."

Will eased her away from him. "How old are you?" he asked.

"Seventeen," she replied as she wiped her eyes.

Will smiled warmly in a way that reminded her of Chandler. "Same as me."

"How old is your—your brother?" she wondered aloud.

"Twenty-four," Will replied. "But when he hasn't had any blood for a while, he gets a little wrinkled."

Stacey sighed. "My God. I can't believe that I was ready to let him—" She shuddered from head to toe.

"I told you, he put the whammy on you. Jeez,

you saw the coffin and the way he backed off when I flashed this."

He showed her the cross again.

"How did Chandler become like this?" Stacey asked.

It was Will's turn to sigh. "We grew up on Long Island. When Chandler was twenty, there was this older woman. She drew him in the same way he was controlling you."

"But he wasn't going to kill me," Stacey said. "He was going to make me be like him."

Will regarded her with a discerning expression. "And you'd prefer that to death?"

Stacey's body shook with a glacial chill. She had almost become a vampire—willingly! No, not willingly—Chandler had exerted a force against her. She had been under his influence.

"He really *is* a vampire," she said sadly.

Will took her hand in a consoling gesture. "I know he had you, honey, but he's left a girl like you behind in every town that he's visited. This is his fifth stop on the trail."

Stacey scowled at him. "What do you mean, a girl like me?"

Will exhaled and looked at the dark road. "Five towns, five girls left in lunatic asylums. Mental hospitals."

"What?"

"They don't die, Stacey, but they go crazy. They don't seem to turn into full-fledged vampires. But they can't survive in a normal environment. They just go nuts."

"That could have been me," Stacey said, a hand to her throat. "But why would Chandler do this?"

"I think he's building up a network," Will replied. "Girls strung all over the country. When he wants to return to a town where he's done his predator thing, he can break her out and have her lure in victims."

"No!"

He looked at her, his green eyes glowing in the sudden headlights of an oncoming car. "Believe it, Stacey. This isn't some loverboy you're dealing with here. This guy is for real. And you almost bought the whole package."

She hung her head. How could she have been so stupid? Chandler had drawn her in, had almost sucked the life right out of her.

"Don't be so hard on yourself," Will told her.

She drew a deep breath. "Will?"

"Yeah, honey?"

"Thanks for saving me," Stacey said, turning to look at him. "I mean it."

"Let's get you home," Will suggested. "And don't worry. I'm not going to let him get you tonight. By the way, has he been in your house yet?"

"Yes. Why?"

Will grimaced. "Once you invite a vampire to come in, he's got the run of the place. But, hey,

I can take care of that. Nothing that a cross and some garlic can't cure."

Stacey shuddered again. This couldn't be happening. It had to be some sort of dream.

"Home," Will urged.

Stacey put the car in gear and took off for her place. They were silent as the Tracker wound through the curving streets of Prescott Estates. Stacey was numb, nearly paralyzed by the bizarre events of the evening. Would she be able to sleep tonight? she wondered.

Stacey turned the corner, braking as soon as she saw the police car parked on the street. "Oh no!"

"Don't tell me," Will said. "That cop is parked in front of your house!"

"Yes—"

Will sighed. "Okay, you're going to need an alibi."

"An alibi?"

"Just listen," he told her, "this is what you're going to say. . . ."

Stacey's stomach turned cartwheels as she opened the front door of her house. The police officer was waiting with her father and mother. Stacey took short breaths, hoping that she could maintain her composure. Will had been against telling the police about Chandler. Stacey hoped that his plan would work.

Mr. Linden stood up, rushing toward her.

"Stacey, where have you been? You weren't in your room."

Mrs. Linden looked rattled. "We were so worried about you, honey. There's been another death. A young girl about your age. We were worried sick that it might be—oh, I don't want to think about it." Her mother shivered.

The police officer nodded to Stacey. "Evening, miss."

Stacey tried to smile. "I had to go back to school to get some books from my locker." She held up the books that had been in the Tracker all along.

"Your mother was correct when she said there's been another death," the police officer said. "Were you acquainted with the boy who hanged himself?"

Stacey nodded, bowing her head. "Yes, it was tragic."

"We think the dead girl is named Millie Johnson," the officer went on. "She was found about an hour ago outside the gazebo at the park. Did you know her, Miss Linden?"

Stacey looked up. "Millie? Yes, she was a friend of mine. I used to—well, I used to pay her to do my homework."

The officer's eyes narrowed. "And you dated the Barton boy?"

"Yes," Stacey replied. "A little."

"Where were you tonight?" the cop asked.

Stacey looked at her father. "Is this okay, Dad?"

Mr. Linden nodded. "You have nothing to hide, Princess. Tell the truth."

Stacey hoped that she was coming off as sincere. "Uh, I drove around for a little while. I had a flat tire."

The cop looked at her hands. "You aren't dirty."

"I didn't change it," Stacey replied. "Someone did it for me, this boy. He—"

Just then, a knocking came at the front door.

"Who could that be?" Mr. Linden asked, heading to answer the rapping.

When he opened the door, Will Carr stood on the stoop with a tire iron in hand. "Hello," Will said quickly. "Is Stacey here? She forgot to take this after I helped her change a tire." He thrust the iron at Mr. Linden.

Mr. Linden took the tool and opened the door a little wider. "Come in. It's all right, come on."

Will stepped in, smiling sheepishly. "Hey, Stacey, you forgot something, so I thought I'd bring it on over."

The police officer took out a pad and pencil. "What's your name, son?"

"Will. William Carr. My brother is Stacey's night class teacher. I was out for a walk when I saw that she needed help. I got my hands all dirty, so I better not touch anything."

He held out his hands for the policeman's inspection.

"You from around here?" the officer asked.

"No, I'm visiting my brother from Long Island. Like I said, it really freaked me out when I found out Stacey was one of his students. Small world, huh?"

The cop's eyes fell on Mr. Linden. "You know this teacher?"

Mr. Linden nodded. "Yes, his name is Chandler Carr. He's done wonders with Stacey."

More than wonders, Stacey thought.

"I can vouch for Chandler Carr," Mrs. Linden said.

The officer nodded. "All right, folks. Thanks for everything. I didn't mean to disturb you so late."

"It's quite all right," Mr. Linden replied.

When the police officer had departed, Will gave a goofy smile to everyone. "I better be going. Good night."

Mrs. Linden showed him to the front door. "Thank you so much for helping Stacey."

Helping me? Stacey thought. He *saved* my life.

After Will had gone, Stacey made her excuses and retired to her bedroom. She sat on the bed with the lights out, listening to the wind as it shook the window panes. In a few minutes, someone was tapping at the casement. She feared that Chandler had come for her.

"Open up," Will said in a raspy whisper. "I'm here."

Stacey lifted the window. "Are you coming in?"

"No," Will replied. "Here, take this."

He handed her a wooden cross and a ring of garlic cloves. "Vampire repellant," he told her.

"It stinks!" Stacey said.

"Better than taking a dirt nap," Will replied. "Now, listen—I'm gonna be around, okay."

"Why don't you stay in my room?" Stacey offered.

Will chortled. "Yeah, right. What will your mommy and daddy say if they catch you with a boy in your room?"

"But it's cold out there."

He gave a sigh. "I'll survive."

"Are you sure we shouldn't tell the police?" Stacey asked.

Will shook his head. "No. I tried that once and Bat-boy was out of town before they could search his house."

Stacey sighed. "This is all so crazy."

"Listen, I'll see you tomorrow," Will told her. "We can talk during the day when he's sleeping."

Stacey nodded, shivering in the cool air. "Okay."

Will hesitated, looking up at her from the casement. "Stacey, there's one other thing I want you to do."

"What's that?" she asked hesitantly.

"Help me kill Chandler," Will replied. "It's the only way to stop him."

Stacey could not believe her own reply. "All right, Will. I'll help you kill him."

That night, she slept uneasily, waking to the sound of something tapping against her window. She heard the leathery flutter of wings. But when she raised the cross in front of her, the bat only squealed and flew off into the cold night.

FOURTEEN

The next morning, Stacey awakened with a headache and a strange sense that everything the night before had been a waking nightmare that hadn't really happened. Then she saw the cross lying on the bed beside her. The scent of garlic hung in the air. It was all too real for the brown-haired girl with deep blue eyes.

Stepping to the window, she gazed into the white-laced yard. A light coating of rim-frost had covered Port City during the night. She thought about Will, the good-looking boy who claimed to be Chandler's brother. Had he survived the night? And would he really try to protect her?

A chill spread through Stacey's shoulders. She felt horrible after a restless night. Had she actually agreed to help Will slay his brother? What if Chandler *wasn't* a vampire?

No, Stacey had seen the blood packets and the coffin. She had witnessed the hideous expression on Chandler's face when he threatened Will. Chandler had even admitted to killing Derek and that weirdo Elvin. And he had to be stopped.

Turning away from the window, Stacey walked mindlessly through her morning routine. She dressed for school, forgetting that it was Saturday. When her mother reminded her of that fact at the breakfast table, Stacey excused herself and went out into the backyard. She kept waiting and watching for Will.

When would Will come? And did he have a solid plan for getting rid of his own brother? Stacey kept expecting to wake up in her bed, warm and cozy on a cold day.

She rubbed her arms to ward off the chill. Will wasn't coming. He had left her high and dry. Would Chandler try to hurt her without Will around to protect her?

Chandler had said that he loved her, that he wanted her to enter the dark world of her own volition. She had been under his spell when he made those claims. If Will had been telling the truth, Stacey had come close to ending up in an asylum, raving like a madwoman.

"He's not coming," she said to herself.

As she was turning toward the back door, she heard the voice filtering through the fence. "Hey, gorgeous, right here."

Will Carr vaulted over the fence, darting in Stacey's direction. He carried a backpack on his shoulder. Stacey thought he looked tired. Had he stayed outside all night?

"Did Bat-boy show up last night?" Will asked.

Stacey nodded. "I heard something tapping against the window. Then I flashed the cross you gave me and it left."

"I thought that would work."

"Where did you go?" Stacey asked.

Will sucked in the cold air, exhaling like he was tired and bored. "I hung around for a while. Then I had to split. I needed to get some sleep. I figured the cross would get you through the night. I had to find some other things we're going to need if we plan to kill him."

Stacey shivered. "Kill him?"

Will frowned at her. "You're getting cold feet, aren't you, Stacey?"

"I—I don't know. I mean, we're going to—to murder him. He's a person, Will. He's your brother."

Will shook his head vehemently. "No, he's a monster. I've seen what he does to people. And you have too. What about your boyfriend? Huh? Do you miss ol' Derek?"

She blushed. "That's not fair!"

"Was it fair what Chandler did to him? Huh? What's it going to be, Stacey?"

"You can't talk to me like that!"

Will bristled, but he held his temper. "Stacey, I can't do this alone. I need your help. I've tried to get Chandler for two years now. But he always escapes from me."

Stacey hung her head, feeling a multitude of conflicting emotions. "I just don't know if I can kill someone."

"*I'll* do the killing," Will assured her.

"Why do you need me?" she asked cautiously.

He shivered, rubbing his bare hands together. "Can we get out of the cold to talk about this?"

Stacey ushered Will inside, introducing him again to her mother and father. They seemed pleased that Will had come over. What would they say if they knew what Will and Stacey had in mind for Stacey's night class teacher?

Stacey took Will to her room where the muscular boy dropped his backback on the bed. He took out a long, pointed wooden stake, a piece of netting rolled into a log, several wooden crosses and another bag of garlic. Stacey stared wide-eyed at the sharpened piece of wood.

"What's that for?" she asked.

Will laughed a little. "Haven't you ever heard of the old wooden stake through the heart? It kills the vampires every time. That is, if you can bury it in the chest. It has to go deep. And it was blessed too, by a priest who thought he was blessing a baseball bat for my little brother."

Stacey shook her head slowly. "I can't go through with this, Will. I'm afraid."

"Who isn't? Look, Stacey, Chandler doesn't want me around. He knows I want to kill him. But there is something he wants in Port City. He wants it real bad."

"What?"

Will pointed at her. "*You*. He wants *you*, Stacey."

"No, Will, I—"

"You're the bait," Will went on, ignoring her protestations. "We can draw him out. Then I can—well, you know."

Stacey sighed. "It seems so cruel."

"No more cruel than what he's done to a lot of girls like you, Stacey. He has to be stopped."

"I know!" Stacey said impatiently. "I know."

Will took her shoulders, turning her toward him. "Stacey, I was like you once. Just a high school student. I didn't have a care in the world. Then my brother got turned into a vampire. My mother and father are dead, so when I kill Chandler, I won't have anyone. I'll be all alone. And when I look at a beautiful girl like you, I think about how long it's been since I had a girlfriend. But I can't rest until my brother is stopped."

He was on the verge of tears. He turned his back to her so she could not see the moisture in his eyes. Stacey put her hand on his shoulder. She felt sorry for him. And he was right— Chandler Carr had to be stopped.

"All right, Will. I'll do it."

"We need a piece of paper," Will replied in a cracking voice. "You've got to write him a letter."

Stacey's brow wrinkled. "A letter?"

"It's gonna say that you still want to be with him," Will told her. "Like I said, you're the bait."

"But how will we get it to him?" Stacey asked.

"We're gonna take it to his house," Will replied. "And then we're gonna tape it to his coffin."

Stacey stepped cautiously beside Will as they approached the house on North Division Road. Black clouds swirled overhead, covering the sky above Port City. It was almost dark.

Stacey grabbed Will's arm. "Are you sure about this?"

"It's the only way," he replied. "Come on. Just like I said. Slow and easy."

They finally reached Chandler's house. Stacey could not believe they had been there the night before. The place looked so harmless during the daylight hours. Chandler hadn't fixed the broken portal, so they went inside without any trouble.

Stacey shivered. "I don't want to go into his room."

Will shrugged. "What difference does it make? He can't come out of his coffin. Come on."

Once again, they gazed upon the coffin where the vampire rested during the day.

Will taped Stacey's note to the coffin. "He'll bite on this, I just know it."

"Will, why don't we just open the coffin and expose him to the light of the sun? Won't that kill him?"

Will gestured to the coffin. "Go ahead and try."

Stacey attempted to lift the coffin lid but it wouldn't budge. "It's stuck."

"He seals it from the inside," Will said. "He's no fool."

"Can't we call the police?" Stacey asked.

"No. By the time they got a warrant, Chandler would be gone. Besides, you don't want to know what the police do when you show up telling vampire stories."

A shiver played along Stacey's spine. The note said that she wanted to meet Chandler that night in the gym at Central. It told him that she didn't believe Will, that she really wanted to be with Chandler in the realm of the night. Stacey wondered if the vampire would believe it.

"Let's book out of here," Will said.

"What are we going to do?" Stacey asked.

Will took a deep breath. "Wait for nightfall," he replied. "Vampires always come out after dark."

Stacey sat in the Central Academy gymnasium building in the cold air with Will. They had been waiting for an hour since darkness fell over Port City. Stacey's stomach was tied in knots.

"Will—"

He raised his head. "Ssh, listen."

Stacey listened closely. "It sounds like the wind."

A cool breeze suddenly blew across their faces.

"How can the wind blow inside?" Stacey whispered.

"It can't," Will replied. "He's here, Stacey. Chandler has come for you."

Stacey put a hand to her throat.

She sat in the darkness, holding her breath, awaiting the arrival of the Prince of the Night. . . .

FIFTEEN

Leathery wings flapped overhead in the still, cold air of the Central Academy gymnasium. Will pointed upward. Stacey could see a sliver of light streaking through the hole in a high ventilation window of the gymnasium dome. The bat had come through the opening in the glass. It now streaked through the night rafters of the ceiling structure above them.

Maybe it was a *real* bat, Stacey thought.

But then she heard the thump of human feet as Chandler landed on the hardwood floor of the gym.

Will nodded to her, pointing in the direction of the footsteps.

Chandler was drawing closer.

Stacey wondered if they were both going to die. Chandler was strong in dead body and evil spirit. But they had to try. He couldn't be allowed to feast on the blood of others.

"Stacey?"

Chandler's voice echoed through the hollow pit of the building. His footsteps halted for a moment. Will had told Stacey that Chandler could see very well in the dark. They had to move fast.

"Stacey, I have come as you asked me to. I'm glad you reconsidered, my darling. I hope my brother Will didn't say too many hateful things about me. He's not right in the head, you know."

Stacey hesitated. Will's expression had turned to fear. He nudged her again, nodding his head. She had to go *now* or the plan wouldn't work.

After a deep breath, Stacey stood up, rising from the dark corner of the gym, stepping in the direction of the vampire. Chandler turned immediately to face her. He had heard her steps. Stacey prayed that Chandler couldn't see Will or the piece of netting that was tucked behind Stacey through the strap of a belt.

"I'm here," Stacey replied. "I'm here, Chandler."

She stopped, waiting for him to come to her. His dark eyes were aglow in the shadows. Will had told her *never* to look Chandler directly in the eyes. She focused on the loose white shirt that he wore beneath his overcoat.

"You came," he said softly. "I knew you would be my bride. Kiss me, my loved one!"

Stacey held out her hand, stopping him. "No, Chandler, not yet. I want to talk first."

He put his fingertips on her chin. "Of course, Stacey. Look at me and we'll talk."

Her eyes fluttered as she raised her head to meet his gaze. In an instant, she was transported. She felt her soul flying forth with the freedom that only Chandler could give her. He had hypnotized her into loving him again, casting the spell of *Nosferatu*, the living dead. She would be with him for eternity, locked in a one-room cell without a window.

"I love you, Stacey," Chandler said, brushing his lips lightly against her mouth.

Stacey felt the pointed ends of his protruding teeth on the smooth ridges of her lips. She wanted him to bite her. She wanted to be the ruler of the night.

"Chandler, I've waited so long for this."

Chandler lowered his mouth toward the vein that pulsed in Stacey's thin neck. "I love you, Stacey. You will be mine forever. We shall never part."

His lips were cold when they touched her neck. Stacey flinched and drew back away from him. Chandler smiled. He tried to bring her close again.

Stacey closed her eyes, hearing Will's voice in her head. *Don't look at his eyes.* She took a long breath. Why did she suddenly want to be Chandler's bride again?

He was a *vampire*!

"No!" Stacey cried. "Chandler, I—"

He was too strong. His arms tugged her close to him. Again he lowered his teeth to the skin of her neck.

"I will drink of your life," he said in his lulling tone. "And you will reign with me in another dimension."

Her arms tensed, pushing at him. "Chandler, no!"

"You resist! Look at me, Stacey. Look into my eyes!"

His hand closed on her face. He turned her toward him, peering into her deep blue eyes. Stacey could not resist. His powers were too strong.

"Now, do you want to come with me into the night?" Chandler asked his captive.

Stacey nodded absently. "Yes."

"It will be much easier this time," Chandler said as his teeth fell toward the white nape of Stacey's neck.

Her eyes grew wide when she felt the pointed tips. "No!"

Chandler hesitated when she screamed. His eyes focused over Stacey's shoulder. He felt the netting tucked in her belt.

"What have you done!" he cried.

Just then, Will rushed headlong from the shadows, dragging the other end of the net behind him. Chandler tried to duck away. Stacey grabbed the front of his overcoat, stopping him long enough for Will to cast the net above Chandler's head.

"Stacey!" Will cried.

She fell away, jerking her end of the net. The mesh tightened. Chandler squirmed in their trap. He hissed and roared, struggling with the strength of a bear.

"We got him!" Will cried.

It was just that simple.

Until Chandler decided to transform himself into a vampire bat. The change happened right before Stacey's eyes. She could not believe what she had seen.

The smaller creature fluttered against the netting, trying to fly out. But Will had forseen the possibilities of his brother's evil powers, so the mesh was tiny enough to prevent the bat from escaping. Will and Stacey were able to pull the flapping creature to the gym floor.

Will reached for the stake and the mallet that he carried in his backpack. "This will be easier!" he said to Stacey.

But the bat was no longer there. Chandler had returned to wrestle with his younger brother. The vampire's hand closed on Will's throat as Will tried to raise the mallet above the wooden stake. Chandler swatted with his other hand, knocking the stake in Stacey's direction.

"You cannot kill me, brother!" Chandler cried.

Will's face was turning blue. Stacey picked up the stake in front of her. She dived at Chandler, sinking the point of the stake into the arm that held Will's throat.

A deafening cry of pain issued from Chandler's dark being. Something gushed from the wound. Stacey wondered if the steaming ooze was vampire blood.

Chandler let go of Will. His body shook with agonizing tremors. Stacey could not believe that she had hurt him. But she had to save Will. She could not let Chandler kill again.

Will crawled toward her with his hand out. "The stake!"

Stacey tossed it to him. "Deep!" she cried. "Bury it deep in his chest."

Will fell on top of his brother. He put the stake on the left side of Chandler's chest. But then Will was no longer fighting the shape of a man.

The wolf had appeared suddenly, all teeth and snarls. It grabbed the loose fabric of Will's coat sleeve, barely missing Will's arm. He drew back from the wolf, watching it wriggle out from under the net.

"He's loose!" Stacey cried.

But when the wolf cleared the net, it started

to limp, unable to walk on the injured foreleg that had been Chandler's arm.

Will lunged at the animal, trying to pierce the wolf's heart. The pointed end of the stick caught the wolf's rib cage, but it only grazed the skin, slashing a shallow mark. The wolf yelped and suddenly the bat was there.

Stacey watched as Will tried to pin the flapping creature with the stake. But the bat was too small. And Chandler came back, slamming Will in the chest, knocking the younger boy to the floor. Will hit with a thud, all the air gone from his lungs.

The bat returned, but it could not fly. The wing was damaged. For a moment, the bat fluttered helplessly on the floor. But Chandler wasn't far away.

Stacey still did not comprehend the transformation. It just seemed to happen instantly. There was no sound, except for Chandler scuffling to his feet. His arm hung limply by his side. He peered at Stacey with eyes that seemed duller now.

"You betrayed me," he said.

Stacey was no longer imprisoned by his eyes. "You would have hurt me, Chandler. Like those other girls you left behind. I would have been crazy."

"But I loved you!" Chandler said.

"You lie, Bat-boy!" Will cried.

Chandler glanced in the direction of his brother, hissing through the hideous monster face.

Will came slowly forward with the stake and mallet in hand. Chandler began to cower away. Stacey thought they had a chance now to kill him.

"Nothing personal, brother," Will said. "I'm just going to put you to sleep for a long time."

Chandler lunged toward Stacey, trying to grab her.

But Stacey quickly raised the cross that she had stashed in her back pocket.

Chandler had to fall back, lurching with his dead arm by his side. "Traitor!"

Will attacked again, using the point of the stake as a trusting sword. Chandler knocked him aside, sliding Will across the floor. Then the vampire looked at Stacey, who brandished the crucifix to stop him.

"You will die!" Chandler said.

Stacey held her ground, never budging.

Chandler turned away, heading for the opposite end of the gymnasium, toward the rear exit.

Will staggered to his feet. "I forget how strong he is."

"We've got to call the police," Stacey said.

Will shook his head. "No. He can't fly now. So we've got him."

They heard the gym door opening as Chandler left the building.

"Come on," Will said. "Let's finish him."

Stacey fell in beside him, following the vampire as it fled into the night.

SIXTEEN

"He's running toward the pool," Stacey said.

Will peered at the advancing figure that moved through the shadows. "Why is he going there?"

"Maybe he wants to drown us," Stacey offered.

Will flashed angry green eyes. "Don't joke about that. I can't swim—and Chandler knows it."

Stacey grabbed Will's arm. "Come on, we'll face him together."

Will hesitated. "Stacey—I don't blame Chandler for loving you. I'm in love with you too."

Stacey grimaced. "What?"

Will started forward. "Come on, let's go!"

They ran in the direction of the pool. Chandler ripped a door from the hinges, entering through the opening he had created. Will and Stacey quickly filled the doorway, but when they searched the shadows of the pool building, they could not see Chandler anywhere.

"Great," Will muttered, holding the wooden stake in front of him. "He's gone."

Stacey put a hand to her throat. "No, he's here. I can feel him."

Will drew in the night air. "Okay, slow and steady. Let's sink the pine in Bat-boy."

Will started inching forward, moving toward the pool. He could barely see in the dim light of the room. Stacey followed behind him, keeping her eyes moving from side to side. Chandler could be anywhere, and he was wounded. The vampire would do anything to stay alive.

Stacey heard scratching to her right. "Will, I think there's something—"

The wolf jumped from the shadows, propelled by its good hind legs. Will pivotted with the stake, but he wasn't quick enough. The canine form crashed into his chest. Will grabbed the wolf and they both went headlong over the edge of the pool, splashing in the heated water.

"No!" Stacey cried.

Will couldn't swim. But the wolf was dog-paddling toward the side of the pool. And Will was down for the count.

Stacey had to dive into the water to save Will. She dragged him to the edge of the pool, lifting him onto the concrete. Will gasped for air. He still had the wooden stake in his hand.

The wolf came toward them, limping on three

legs. But it was Chandler's hand that reached down for his younger brother. With other-worldly strength, Chandler lifted Will from the water, dangling him at arm's length.

"You! I curse the day our father and mother had you!" Chandler cried. "You won't live much longer!"

"You!" Will yelled back at him. "You killed Mom and Dad. You slashed their wrists and made it look like suicide. They didn't find much blood with the bodies, Chandler. You killed our own parents. Admit it!"

"All mortals are fools!" Chandler cried. "You cannot understand the ways of the night."

Will raised the stake, but Chandler shook his body with such force that Will lost his grip.

The stake fell in front of Stacey, who clung to the edge of the pool. It floated on the rippling surface of the water. Stacey grabbed the stake and glanced up.

Chandler's leg was right there, just a few inches away. Stacey held on tightly. She swung the point of the stake, burying it in Chandler's calf.

Will dropped back into the water. Chandler screeched and grabbed his leg. The vampire swung in a circle, bellowing sounds that couldn't come from anything human.

Stacey reached for Will. "Hold this."

Thrusting the stake into his grasp, Stacey held him the way she had been taught in first aid class. She pushed off from the edge of the pool and started to swim toward the other side with Will in tow.

"What are you doing?" Will gurgled.

"Getting away from Bat-boy," Stacey replied with graveyard humor. "He can't swim after us and he can't fly."

Chandler reeled in his pain. Steam rose from the leg wound, like gas escaping from a balloon. Stacey pulled Will onto the ladder, forcing him to climb upward. She also lifted herself from the pool. They stood up, gazing at the terrible spectacle on the other side of the water.

"He's hurting," Will said.

Stacey could not take her eyes away from Chandler. "He's—he's going to die."

"Not yet," Will replied, holding up the wooden stake. "We have to put this where his heart used to be. Otherwise, he'd going to get away."

"Where's the mallet?" Stacey asked.

Will nodded toward the water. "At the bottom of the pool."

Stacey bit her lips, trembling, wet and cold. "Can we just stab him with it?"

"We don't have any choice," Will replied. "You still have your cross?"

"No."

Will reached into his back pocket. "Here, take this one. It's small, but it'll keep him off you."

"Aren't we going together?" she asked, grabbing his hand.

Will shook his head. "No. You go that way. We'll come around at him from both angles. You try to drive him toward me with the cross. Okay? You gonna be all right?"

Stacey took a deep breath and kissed him on the cheek. "Let's get it over with."

They stalked the screeching demon from both sides, inching toward Chandler with their protection in hand.

Chandler stiffened when he saw Stacey approaching. His eyes were dull now. His face had taken on a yellow pallor. Gone was the caring expression of the man she had fallen for— Chandler now had a desperate appearance about him, a wounded beast struggling to survive. And he was still dangerous with his fangs exposed.

Chandler hissed again when she approached him. Stacey raised the cross to back him away. Chandler shuffled with a limp and a dangling arm. Steam rose from both wounds.

"He looks weak," Stacey said.

Will called from behind his vampire brother. "Don't let up. I've got to get this into his chest." Will advanced cautiously, holding the stake in front of him.

Stacey almost pitied Chandler. His face was all wrinkles now as the vapor escaped from his body. Stacey held the cross in front of him. Will made a quick rush in the vampire's direction.

"No!" Stacey cried. "Not yet—"

Chandler wheeled away from the crucifix, reaching out toward Will. The vampire caught the stake in his lethal grip. Will felt the weapon leave his grasp. It fell on the edge of the pool, half submerged on the lip of the pool.

Chandler grabbed Will by the throat again. Will's feet left the concrete surface. Chandler shook him for a moment and then wheeled toward the pool. He was going to drop Will in the water again, so Will would drown.

"No!" Stacey cried.

Chandler dangled Will over the deep end. "When you are dead, I will feast on your blood!"

Stacey watched Chandler drop his brother into the water. She barreled toward the demon, crashing into him, knocking Chandler into the pool with Will. Chandler sank straight down, taking his younger brother with him.

"Will!" She wasn't sure if she should dive in after them. Chandler was strong. He might drown both of them. But she had to do something to save Will. "The stake!"

She glanced around in the dim light. The sharpened stake bumped in the lap of the water. Stacey picked up the weapon and looked back into the pool.

The wolf surfaced, but Will was not beside it.

Stacey braced herself, holding the stake in both hands.

Chandler pulled himself onto the pool ladder

with one arm. His eyes were glowing again. Had he taken some of Will's blood?

"I must kill you now," he said in a raspy tone. "Then I will feed on both of you."

"You aren't feeding on anyone, Chandler—"

He started to laugh at her, cackling like an old woman. His foot came up on the ladder. He started to vault himself onto the concrete ledge.

Stacey ran forward, launching her body into the air. Chandler had not expected the attack. The vampire's chest was exposed, vulnerable to the stake.

The point of the weapon caught the vampire squarely in the hollow of the heart. Stacey fell to the deck, crawling backward to get away from the horrible sound that issued from the monster. Chandler tried to pull out the stake, but it was wedged too deeply.

His face looked straight at her for a painful moment. "I loved you," Chandler uttered, offering his last words.

"I loved you too," Stacey replied.

His body seemed to dissipate, evaporating like dry ice in a sea of saltwater. Chandler was suddenly gone. No trace of him remained beyond the strange smell that thickened the steamy air of the pool building.

"Will!"

Stacey dived into the water, pulling Will's body out of the pool. He wasn't breathing. She turned him on his side, whacking his chest so the water would come out.

"Don't die on me, friend," she said softly.

Stacey tried mouth-to-mouth breathing, filling his lungs with air. She pounded on his chest a few times to start his heart beating. Will didn't respond. He just lay there, limp.

"Come on," Stacey pleaded. "We came too far together for you to die, Will. Please—"

Pressing her lips to his, she blew air into his lungs again.

Suddenly, Will coughed and started to breathe.

In a few seconds, he opened his eyes. "Chandler?" he asked weakly.

Stacey lowered her head. "I killed him."

Will nodded slowly and closed his eyes.

They wouldn't figure out exactly what to do until it was almost daybreak.

EPILOGUE

Stacey startled when the lunch tray dropped in front of her on the table. She glanced up to see Will Carr standing before her. He had appeared all of a sudden in the Central Academy cafeteria. He plopped down in a chair and flashed his green eyes in Stacey's direction.

"Hi, gorgeous," he said in a smooth voice. "Chased any vampires lately?"

Stacey blushed. "Will! What are you doing here? "

He shrugged. "Eating lunch, Miss Linden. Is there anything wrong with that?"

Stacey shook her head. "Where have you been? I haven't seen you since—well, you know."

"Since we slayed Count Dracula," Will replied.

Stacey leaned over the table. "Shh! Do you want everyone to hear?"

"What difference does it make? Who'd believe

that we killed a vampire a week ago? Besides, there's no evidence. No body. My long-lost brother just evaporated into space."

She slumped back in her chair, studying Will as he dug into the tray of meatloaf and potatoes. Had his eyes always been that shade of green? Stacey hadn't remembered him being so handsome, though she now recalled some things he had said when they were fighting Chandler in the dead of night.

"What did you do with the coffin?" Stacey asked.

He chewed, looking up, swallowing before he spoke. "I went back to Chandler's place, just like we said. I found all of his papers. I typed up a document that said he wanted me to handle some of his affairs for him. I faked his signature pretty good. Turns out I didn't even need it."

"But the coffin?" she insisted.

"Funeral home. They paid cash for it. Two thousand bucks. Said it was worth ten grand, but I didn't care. I told them my brother had been a host for a late-night horror movie television show back in New York. They were convinced that he had just kept the coffin for a gag. I had to take out the dirt though. That was pretty creepy."

Stacey suddenly didn't want any more of the wilted salad on her tray. "Wow. What about the blood packets?"

"Burned them," Will replied. "I got rid of his

books too. Nobody even questioned me about them. I gave them away. They weren't any good to me. Nothing of his matters now, except . . ." His voice trailed off.

"Except what?"

"The money," Will replied. "Chandler had all the money my parents left after he killed them. Turned everything into cash. I found it. Over a hundred grand."

"Where—where is it?" Stacey asked.

He smiled. "In a safe place. How are you doin'? Any nightmares or anything?"

She sighed deeply. "At first, especially the next day. But it's getting better."

"Anybody notice you were having a rough time?" he asked in a tone of genuine concern.

"Yes, but I just told them to leave me alone. You know, Will, it's funny. In a way, your brother helped me. I'm doing okay in all of my subjects. I wonder if he really cared about me?"

Will dropped his fork and leaned back. "I used to know a Chandler who was a pretty good guy. Maybe some of that was left inside him."

Stacey glanced suddenly to her left and right, like she was looking for someone. "I hope Mr. Kinsley doesn't see you in here. It's against the rules to have visitors during school hours."

"Relax, gorgeous, I enrolled in Central, first thing this morning. I'm an official student."

Stacey's jaw dropped. "You're going to Central now?"

"I need an education," Will replied. "Besides, I got a room near here. I plan to start my life over now that Chandler is gone. Port City seems like a good place. There aren't any vampires around here, not anymore." He grinned.

Stacey smiled back. "You know, when we were chasing your brother, you said something interesting, Will."

He picked up his fork. "Yeah, what was that?"

"You said you were in love with me," Stacey replied. "Is that true?"

It was his turn to blush and look away. "Hey, you kissed me, Stacey. Didn't you?" He glanced up to meet her gaze.

Stacey exhaled and shook her head. "What are we going to do?"

"Be friends?" Will suggested.

Stacey's brow wrinkled. "Hey, what are you telling everyone about your brother? I mean, he can't just disappear. Can he?"

"He was used to moving on quick," Will told her. "He kept a letter all ready to send to his bosses. He had a reputation for jumping around, but he was able to use his powers to get people to hire him for night classes. I sent the letter off a few days ago. So if anybody asks, I don't know where he is and I decided to stay in Port City."

Stacey leaned back, eyeing him. "So, you're in love with me?"

"Yeah, what of it? You busy on Saturday? We could go out!"

Stacey told him she'd think about it.

WELCOME TO CENTRAL ACADEMY . . .

It's like any other high school on the outside.
But inside, fear stalks the halls —
and terror is in a class by itself.

———————

Please turn the page for a sneak preview of the next
TERROR ACADEMY book —
don't miss SCIENCE PROJECT!

Andrea Hill's dark brown eyes were focused on a group of her friends as they played volleyball on Hampton Way Beach. Summer was almost over for Andrea and the rest of the students who would soon become the junior class at Central Academy. The summer vacation had been fun for Andrea, up until now at least. She had been dating Johnny Randall, a popular boy who would no doubt be the starting quarterback for the Central football squad as soon as classes began.

Andrea sighed and leaned back against the top of the picnic table. Her smooth hand absently brushed away the long, thick mane of black hair that fell onto her bare shoulders. She was dressed for the beach in a green bathing suit top and a pair of cutoff jeans. Her tall, slender body had been covered with sunscreen to avoid tanning like some of the other girls. Andrea was considered quite attractive by all of the boys in her class. She could've dated anyone, but she had chosen Johnny for reasons that were becoming less important with each passing day.

Andrea reached back toward the table, grabbing her sunglasses. She covered her dark eyes with the polarized lenses. Her cleft chin tilted in the direction of the volleyball game again. Johnny spiked the ball into the sand, leaping higher than any of the others in the competition. He clapped his hands, gazing at Andrea with a knowing wink.

Andrea shivered, even though the day was warm and humid. Johnny had been quite the gentleman—at first. But he was building toward something and Andrea was fairly certain that she knew that he wanted from her.

Johnny pointed a finger in her direction. "You and me, babe. Later. Okay?"

Andrea ignored him, looking away. The sun beat down on her high cheekbones and upturned nose, prompting her to use more sunscreen. She also ran the blunt end of a lip protectant over her generous mouth. Andrea didn't want her skin to look like leather.

"Got some more of that, Andrea?"

Suzy Clements, a casual friend, sat down next to Andrea. Suzy was a full-figured girl with green eyes and reddish hair. She wasn't as pretty or as popular as Andrea, but the in-crowd accepted her because she had a car and her parents' house in Prescott Estates was equipped with a swimming pool.

Andrea handed her the sunscreen, sighing. "Sure, take all you want. We won't be needing it after school starts."

Suzy glanced sideways at her. "You sound bummed. What's wrong? Is it Johnny?"

Yes, Andrea said to herself.

"You're lucky," Suzy went on, not waiting for an answer. "He's a major babe. I wish a guy like that would come after me."

Suzy started to rub sunscreen on her thick legs. Like a lot of people in the loose, fast-running popular crowd, Suzy thought only of herself and her own needs and wants. To Suzy, Johnny was a prize to be won or lost, a hunk with a cool car and a muscular body—the big quarterback. Andrea, however, had an entirely different view of her boyfriend.

A cry of dismay echoed from the volleyball game. Andrea watched as the white ball rolled in her direction. She picked it up and lifted her face to see Johnny coming toward her.

Johnny posed in front of her, flexing his muscles. "That puke Chaz is going to pay for spiking me!"

Andrea held out the ball to him. "I'm sure."

"You and me, later." Johnny turned back to the net. "Hey, Chaz, you're dog meat!"

Johnny swaggered back to the game. He was cute with his bright jammer shorts and long sandy hair. His blue eyes had white rings in the irises, giving him a predatory gaze that sometimes unnerved Andrea. She watched as Johnny ranked on Chaz Elliot. Although Chaz was supposed to be Johnny's best friend, they always seemed to be fighting.

After a heated exchange between them, the game resumed. But Andrea was so bored by the competition that she couldn't concentrate enough to care. Her brown eyes wandered back to the blue sky that seemed so perfect over the Port City area. It should have been the perfect place for an end of the summer party—rolling dunes, sandy beachfront, natural seaside vegetation and flocks of seagulls turning overhead. But somehow, Andrea couldn't enjoy it on this sunny afternoon.

"What's your problem?" Suzy asked in a casual tone. "Are you and Johnny fighting?"

No, but we're probably *going* to be fighting, Andrea thought.

"I'm okay," Andrea replied. "I'm just bummed that summer is over. That's all."

Suzy sighed. "I know what you mean. I was hoping I'd get a real boyfriend this summer, like you have."

"Yeah, he's a real boyfriend all right," Andrea muttered under her breath. "Real trouble is more like it."

"Huh?" Suzy asked numbly.

Andrea suddenly became impatient. "Shut up, Suzy. Just rub your fat thighs and leave me alone."

Suzy blushed, lowering her eyes to the sand at their feet. Suzy was always taking abuse about her weight from the others. But it was part of the price she paid to hang with the in-crowd, the popular set at Central. They had all been together since middle school, the jocks, the jokers, the cheerleaders and the hangers-on—and the beautiful girls like Andrea, who were envied by the less fortunate geeks who sat home on Friday nights.

"You didn't have to say that," Suzy said softly. "I mean, I expect it from the others. But not you, Andrea. You've always been nice to me."

Andrea took a deep breath, exhaling, gazing at the sky. She felt horrible about what she had said to Suzy. There was no excuse for being abusive, even if Johnny and his bunch were inclined to put-downs and derisiveness.

"I know I'm overweight," Suzy started, "but that's no reason for you to—"

Andrea reached out, touching Suzy's shoulder. "Hey, I'm sorry. It's just—I don't know."

Suzy turned and nodded. "It's okay."

"Suzy—it's—"

Andrea stopped short of confiding in Suzy. How could she tell anyone that she was thinking about breaking up with Johnny? He was the center of their clique, the hub at the spoke of the wheel. They'd all laugh at her, or shun her. After all, Andrea ruled as their queen, standing beside King Johnny.

"How shallow it all is," Andrea said absently.

"What?" Suzy asked.

Andrea sighed again. "Come on, let's go feed the birds."

"Sure," Suzy replied with a weak smile.

They grabbed two bags of pretzels and started away from the picnic table.

"Hey! Where you goin'?"

Andrea wheeled in the direction of Johnny's expectant tone. The volleyball game had stopped for the moment. Johnny stood there in the sand with his hands on his hips, glaring at Andrea with his wolfish blue eyes.

"Where do you think you're goin', Foxy?" Johnny asked in a rough tone. "I didn't give you permission to leave."

Everyone laughed. All of their so-called "friends" were having a good chuckle at Andrea's expense. Instead of censuring Johnny for acting like a Neanderthal, they were expecting Andrea to bow to her master's command. The queen always had to obey the king—wasn't that part of the popular crowd scene?

"I'm going to feed the birds," Andrea replied curtly. "And I don't need your permission to do it."

Johnny looked stunned for an instant, but then he grimaced and waved at her. "I love a woman that stands up to me. You and me, babe. Later! Hey, make sure Chubbo doesn't eat all the pretzels!"

Everyone at the party enjoyed another laugh aimed at Andrea and Suzy. They turned and walked away. Andrea wasn't sure how much longer she could take their insensitivity. Why had her attitude toward them changed so quickly, almost overnight?

Suzy fell in beside her, waddling along in the sand. "I know what's wrong with you, Andrea."

"Oh? Then tell me," Andrea quipped.

"You hate them," Suzy replied. "You hate them almost as much as I do."

Andrea glanced sideways at the chubby girl. "Hate them?"

"You're smarter than they are, Andrea," Suzy said with a sudden burst of insight. "I am too. But if I leave them, what would I have? But you're better than Johnny. And I know what he's trying to do. He *did* it to me!"

Andrea kept walking toward the dunes. "I don't want to hear this, Suzy."

"But Andrea, Johnny and I—"

"No!"

Andrea stopped near the dunes, tearing open the bag of pretzels. She started to throw them in the air, attracting a squadron of seagulls in an instant. The white and gray yellow-beaked birds beat their wings, catching bits of pretzels and diving to snag the ones that fell into the sand.

Suzy grabbed Andrea's shoulders, turning her away from the squawking flock of gulls.

"You have to listen to me, Andrea. Johnny used me. He uses everyone. He—"

"Shut your fat mouth, Clements!"

Johnny was there all of a sudden, pushing Suzy so hard that she fell into the sand.

"Don't let him use *you*!" Suzy cried.

Johnny grabbed Andrea's arm. "Don't listen to this lying blob, foxy. She's got some imagination."

"He's lying," Suzy insisted. "Don't believe him."

Andrea tried to pull away from his grip. "Let go of me, Johnny. I mean it!"

But the muscular boy was too strong. "Come on, foxy. You're going with me."

Johnny began to drag Andrea toward the shadows of the dunes.